THE
Rule Breaker

USA TODAY BESTSELLING AUTHOR
RENEE HARLESS

Editing by Hot Tree Editing

Cover photo by Shutterstock

Cover design by Porcelain Paper Designs

Reader group: Renee Harless' Risque Readers
https://www.facebook.com/groups/reneeharlessrisquereaders/
Facebook: facebook.com/authorreneeharless
Amazon: www.amazon.com/Renee-Harless/e/B00VAHGAWE
Bookbub: www.bookbub.com/authors/renee-harless
Newsletter: www.reneeharless.com/newsletter
Instagram: @Renee_harless
Twitter: @Renee_harless
Snapchat: @renee_harless

THE
Rule Breaker

USA TODAY BESTSELLING AUTHOR
RENEE HARLESS

Dedicated to my Risque Readers.

CHAPTER ONE
Quinn

*T*HE CAR JOSTLES ME back and forth as it jerks with every bump and hole in the road. Nope, this isn't the worn-down country road you're imagining. It's a four-lane major highway heading toward my destination—home. A place I haven't stepped foot into in the past six years.

Another bump knocks the water bottle from my lips and onto my lap, soaking through my white denim shorts.

Great.

"Fuckity, fuck, fuck," I screech, bopping in the seat as the cool water flows into each tiny crevice of my legs and clothing.

A horn honks loudly from the car next to me, and I look up hastily to swerve back into my lane. My chest heaves as I gather air in my lungs, my knuckles turning white against the black leather steering wheel.

Needing a moment to gather myself, I veer the car over to the shoulder, moving across the other lane of traffic. The car, of course, hits another deep pothole, and I pray the tire doesn't burst from the impact.

Finally situated on the side of the road, I snag my sweatshirt from the back and place it under myself on the seat. Unfortunately, I can do little about my wet shorts. Hopefully when I arrive at Izzy's place she'll have a fresh pair I can slide on before I unpack. Or, which is more likely, they'll be somewhat dry by the time I arrive.

My best friend, Izzy, is the only reason I plan to return to our town just outside of Houston, Texas. When my agent suggested that I get a little rest and relaxation before I start filming my next movie, I had no intention of leaving Los Angeles, California. LA is my home now, but the very night my agent Priscilla made her suggestion, I was jolted out of bed when a box crashed to the floor in my closet. Once I had finally calmed down and made sure there wasn't anyone trying to attack me in my condo, I had discovered my box of photo albums had been the offending item to scare me shitless. And when I investigated further, walking amongst the scattered images, my gaze landed on a picture of myself, my best friend, and her brother.

It had been from my first summer in Dale City, Texas. My family had up and moved two weeks prior when my dad's job relocated, and I was ecstatic to learn that there was a girl my age living across the street, I had visions of us being the best of friends, as close as sisters, because I had no siblings. When I found out that she had a brother, my body turned into a permanent piece of petrification. Coming from an all-girls middle school, my experience with boys was very limited. Clothing, makeup, hair? I knew nothing of it. My mom and dad were doctors who lived in scrubs and counted their days by the surgeries they had scheduled.

But the day the moving truck pulled into the driveway, a bouncing ponytail of curls made its way toward me and enveloped my body in a hug so tight I was scared that I was being kidnapped. A boy about a foot taller than me had shown up moments later and pried the girl's arms off my body, and I gasped for air as he stood there with narrowed eyes. Izzy had introduced herself as I was held captive by the boy's eyes, and then she explained that his name was Trevor. I had rolled his name around in my head a few times and decided that it matched his appearance. He was equally mysterious and alluring. And at thirteen, I instantly developed my first real crush as my heart pitter-pattered in my chest beneath his gaze.

Izzy and I had been inseparable as teenagers, though we were nothing alike in looks or personality except for our blonde hair. She was the head cheerleader while I had been the president of the drama club. But our friendship never wavered.

The moment my gaze came across the picture in my closet, I knew I could take the next month away from LA and go back home. I hadn't seen Izzy since her last trip out during the summer, and that had been almost a year ago. It had been too long.

Veering back onto the highway, my phone chimes with an incoming call. As if knowing I was thinking about her, Izzy's voice echoes in the car as I connect the call through the stereo. My car is too old for one of those new Bluetooth setups, much to my agent's dismay, but I can still talk handsfree with a bit of wiring work.

"Are you here yet?" Izzy cries out.

"No, not yet. I'm like an hour outside of Houston," I claim, peering at the green sign as I pass.

"I can't believe you've driven the whole way. That's like a hundred hours."

"Twenty-one to be exact, but you know I'm used to going on very little sleep."

"I just can't wait for you to get here. An entire month with my bestie. And I have a surprise planned."

Oh no. I hated Izzy's surprises. First it was letting her choose my high school schedule. Art class and I did not mix. Then I let her choose our prom dresses. Chartreuse looked great on her tan skin, not so much on my porcelain coloring. Finally, she surprised me with a graduation party at my house when my parents were away at a medical convention. You can imagine when little loner me walked into a party and no one knew who I was. And in typical fashion, my parents came home a day early from the convention to find me and Izzy passed out on the couch.

"Izzy, I don't think that's such a good idea. You remember what happened last time." That very night is the reason I haven't touched an ounce of alcohol in six years. It was also the night that solidified my move away from Dale City. Two weeks later, I up and left without so much as a goodbye to my best friend.

"It's going to be fine, Quinn. Don't be a party pooper. You're only young once."

A tractor trailer honks as he passes, and I return my focus to the road in front of me instead of on my growing anxiety.

"Izzy, I need to go. I'll be there soon."

An hour later, I pull off the highway and make my way toward home. The strip malls closest to the highway give way to the sidewalk-lined neighborhoods of Dale City. The town is big enough to get lost in but small enough that most people know who you are in some fashion. Both a blessing and a curse.

I drive up to a small white ranch-style home, a complete contrast to my loud and outspoken best friend. Glancing down at my phone, I verify that I have the correct address before I turn off the car.

Here we go.

Stepping out of the car, I let the humid heat move over me. Summer in Texas is no joke, the sweat is already beading on the back of my neck causing the fine hairs to curl on their ends. Moving around toward the back of the car, I pull out the duffel bag I stuffed there in my hasty retreat to leave LA, and also snag the few copies of the script I need to work on while I take this mini vacation.

Suddenly I feel a pair of eyes on me, but as I look around the neighborhood, I don't find anyone openly gazing at me. Shrugging the duffel bag higher on my shoulder, I lock my car and make my way to the front door.

My hand is poised at the door, anticipating knocking, when it swings open widely and I find myself crushed by two thin arms wrapped around me. The hug reminds me of the first time I met Izzy, and I can't help returning the gesture.

"I can't believe you're here! I never thought you'd come back to Dale City, especially since you're this 'world-famous actress' now," she air quotes, giving me a small reprieve to breathe.

I blush from her compliment. She's not incorrect. I had very little intention of ever returning to the town that rarely paid me any attention.

"Come on, I have your room ready," she instructs as she tugs me into her house.

My eyes roam the space, the neutral décor giving way to pops of color. This is the Izzy I had come to love like a sister. She is equally calm as she is spunky.

"We'll grab the rest of your bags later. Right now I want to catch up," she adds as she opens a door to a small guest room. The walls are a subtle blue, almost gray in tint. A bed sits between two windows overlooking the backyard, covered in a blue paisley duvet.

I slide my duffel from my arm and place it on the bed, then rifle around for a pair of yoga shorts. My current shorts have dried, but now they're itchy and uncomfortable.

"I'm going to change really quick. My shorts are feeling funny since I spilled a water bottle on them earlier."

"Sure, the bathroom is down the hall to the left."

"Thanks."

Once I situate myself in dry clothing, I make my way back to the bedroom and find Izzy resting casually against the headboard with a Dr. Pepper waiting for me.

I haven't had soda in years, not since I left. Truthfully, I haven't had much that would be considered unhealthy in the last six years, so I groan the moment the bubbly liquid touches my lips. It fizzles down my throat, and I unsurreptitiously belch as it settles in my stomach.

Placing the cap back on the bottle, I put it on the nightstand and crawl beside Izzy on the bed.

Her eyes rake my body up and down before she meets mine. "You look good, Quinn. California obviously agrees with you."

"Thanks. I really love it there. All the people, and there's always something going on."

Izzy smiles, but I can tell by the way her eyes don't crinkle in the corner that she's forcing it.

"What's going on, Iz?"

She takes a swig of her own Dr. Pepper and I watch as she gulps it down. She straightens her back and moves to sit cross-legged on the bed.

"I had always hoped you would hate it there and move back home. Of course, that's a terrible thing to think for your bestie. And when you told me that after a month of being there, you had gotten the lead in that movie, I prayed it would bomb. But it didn't, of course. You were amazing in it, and you're amazing in all of the movies."

"Izzy, I had no idea. Why didn't you say anything?"

"Because I'm your best friend and I never wanted to hurt you. Plus I knew your parents made it hard to come back."

My parents. That's a sticky situation in itself.

"Do you plan on seeing them while you're home?" she asks.

"I don't intend to, but I do want to stop by the house at some point. And Izzy, I'm sorry I didn't make an effort to visit you more. I haven't been the best friend in the world."

Flicking her hand in the air, she lets our troubles fall by the wayside.

"You're an award-winning actress. None of us ever really expected you to come back. I'm just glad I get you for a little while."

Leaning over, I rest my head on her shoulder and she rests hers on top of my head. It reminds me of a time when we were inseparable and innocent.

"So tell me, what's this surprise?" I question as I take a deep breath, letting the damp, cool air from the central air system fill my lungs.

"Well, I was thinking we could go out tonight and celebrate your being home. We'll get dressed up and everything."

I eye her skeptically. The last thing I remember is there was only one bar in town, and it wasn't a place for young girls to visit. Hopefully that's changed.

"Where did you want to go? I didn't really bring any dressy clothes with me."

"Don't worry. You'll just need shorts and boots. The stereotypical Texan outerwear."

I hate to tell her that I haven't unboxed my cowboy boots since I packed them up years ago. When I moved to LA, I took my entire savings from working at the vet's office while in high school—after purchasing my car, of course—and rented a teeny-tiny studio apartment. I was lucky to get a big break when I did because I would've ended up on the streets soon. California is expensive. After my first movie launched me into stardom, I was able to afford a larger condo. During that move, I just shoved the box onto the upper shelf of my closet with everything else that reminded me of home.

"And where will we be going exactly?" I ask as I move off the bed and start unpacking my duffel bag of travel clothes.

"It's a bar downtown called Sidewinders. It's new, and every once in a while they have a band that plays. Come on, Quinny, don't be a hermit."

I chuckle as she leaves her spot on the bed and stomps her foot heavily on the ground. Leave it to a twenty-four-year-old to throw a tantrum like a toddler.

"I'll go, but I need a nap first. And don't call me Quinny. You know I hate that."

"Ok, nap. I'll leave you alone, but first I have one quick question for you."

Prickles tingle along my neck as she grabs the shirt I'm folding from my grasp and tosses it on the bed.

"Look at me, Quinn."

I take a minute to gather my thoughts before I twist my head to gaze over at her. I knew this question was coming, and when she would visit in California I was always able to escape her scrutiny. Here, now, I'm stuck with no way out.

"You're my best friend. Why haven't you asked me about my family."

"How are your parents?"

"Good, but I'm not dumb. Ask again."

"Izzy, how is your brother?"

"That's better. Trevor is Trevor. And I seriously hope and pray that you've gotten over that crazy crush you had growing up, because he's still the captain of the douchecanoe team."

"Douchecanoe team?"

She waves her hand in frustration. "A team of douchebags. Come on, I know you've heard it. Anyway, don't worry. I'm sure he'll be too busy working to be around much. You're supposed to be home to rest and relax."

"And read through my script."

"Yes, and read through your script. He promised to be on his best behavior."

"Best behavior? He was never cruel to me. He was just… dismissive, that's all."

Trevor was always good at ignoring me as a teenager, and I never really knew why. Though I always supposed it was because I didn't mix with his group of rebels and that he always saw me as his little sister, much to my dismay.

"Well, whatever it is, he's going to leave us alone so I can cherish my time with my bestie. Go take your nap and be ready to leave by eight."

"Got it."

I haven't really thought of Trevor in years. With my celebrity status, I didn't have any personal social media accounts, just ones that were run by my publicist, so I havn't seen or heard from him since I left. And when I would speak with Izzy, we kept our conversation light and drama free.

As I lie in bed, I think about Trevor and know that my childhood crush probably looks just as handsome now as he did then; there's no way the infamous Trevor Shaw could be anything else. He had been my best friend just as much as Izzy, the three of us inseparable. He was always good about listening to me vent my adolescent troubles without adding any words of wisdom; he would just take me in.

Then one day that changed, and I never knew what happened. He wouldn't say hi to me in the halls if we passed in school, or walk with me and Izzy to the ice cream shop in town. It never seemed to bother Izzy—she seemed more pleased about it than anything—but it had hurt me to lose him as a friend.

While I'm home, I should reach out to him. Find out what happened. The closure would be good, will help me move on when I go back to LA. Because let's face it, how often does someone get the chance to prove someone wrong?

RENEE HARLESS

CHAPTER TWO
Quinn

I TUG THE LIGHTLY worn brown leather up to my calves and smile. The pink etching of flowers looks exactly like I remember from when Izzy and I picked them out during the summer between our junior and senior years in high school.

I stand in front of the full-length mirror attached to the back of the door and twist back and forth. My denim shorts ride high on my leg, exposing the underside of my bottom. Not enough to be considered scantily clad, but exposing the hard work I've put in at the gym for the past few years. My white tank top scoops low on my chest, exposing the top of my breasts pushed up high from my bra. It skims down my waist, resting just below my navel, exposing the taut muscles of my midriff.

I hear the door creak open just as I move to the dresser to grab my license and cash for the bar.

"Wow, Quinn. You look amazing. No one in town is going to recognize you."

Of course not. I'm not the frumpy girl with frizzed hair wearing oversized T-shirts.

"Izzy, I've been on more magazines than I can count. I'm sure a few have found their way into town."

"Yeah, but you know us. We all thought they were photoshopped like most pictures of celebrities. But it's obvious yours haven't been."

I bite down on my lip at her compliment. It's always been my struggle. My skin is thicker than the Webster's dictionary, and I can take critiques and ridicule with the best of them, but hand me a compliment and I freeze up. My publicist tried to get me to take classes for the fear, but it never helped.

"Thanks, Iz. Is it time to go?"

"Yep. I figured we can grab something to eat on the way."

I shut my bedroom door and follow her out of the house toward her small red Honda Civic. It actually surprises me to see her still driving the same car from high school considering her family is wealthy. But that's one of my favorite things about Izzy. She never flaunted her money; none of her family did.

As we start to head out of the neighborhood and down the main street, I relax back into the cloth seat. After my family moved us around every couple of years, Dale City was the first place we all seemed to settle. It was home.

I close my eyes and let the breeze flowing through the open window wisp around me. The smell of the overgrown wheat and corn fields reminds me of the times Izzy, Trevor, and I snuck out of our homes in the darkness of night and ran through the fields toward a small clearing. It was nights like that when we weren't separated by cliques or standards placed by our schoolmates. We were just best friends relaxing under the stars. Then we turned sixteen and everything changed — boyfriends, girlfriends, plays. Our trips to the field became few and far between.

"Whatcha thinking about?"

I turn my gaze toward Izzy and smile. "Just remembering all the times we snuck out to the clearing on the farm." I let out a small laugh. "Remember when we snuck the bottle of Boone's Farm and Trevor brought the Jack Daniel's?"

"Oh my God," she exclaims as she smacks her hand on the steering wheel and giggles. "We were so sick the next day, but no one suspected anything. They thought we had a stomach bug. Man, I can't believe we got away with that."

"That was one of the best nights of my life. I think it was the last time all three of us were together."

"Well that settles it. Before you head back to LA, all three of us are going to have a fun-filled night in the clearing."

"That would be fun, but I seriously doubt your brother will want to join us. I'm sure he'll be busy with his harem like in school."

"Harem?"

"Yeah, a group of girls following him around like love-sick puppies. The ones who made my life miserable because I was your friend and you were Trevor's sister."

"Oh, hmm. He's changed a bit, no harem following him around. But he still has a constant carousel of women."

The car slows, and I recognize the glowing red and white sign.

"I'm surprised this place is still here."

"The Dairy Queen is an institution and place where many fun nights begin. Are you too good for the DQ Lounge now?"

"What? No. I was just surprised, that's all." I glance up at the drive-thru menu and my mouth instantly waters. It's been ages since I've eaten anything greasy. "I'll take a cheeseburger and a milkshake please."

Izzy smiles brightly and whoops in her seat before she places the order. We park the car in the back of the lot and unwrap our burgers. I let out a moan when the juicy hamburger meat touches my tongue. My taste buds instantly react to the flavor of the chargrilled goodness.

Izzy's lips wrap around the straw of her milkshake and she laughs before taking a sip. "I haven't heard moans like that since my last boyfriend."

A cough erupts from my chest, startling me and causing even more to follow. The coughing lasts for a full minute, which in turn causes my abdomen to cramp up. A painful side effect of breathing down the wrong pipe when you remember a part of your past that you wish you hadn't.

Alex Cruz was my first real boyfriend and made sure that when we dated, he used my name to its finest degree. He had been the first actor I dated in Hollywood and used his good looks and influence to convince me that he was worth it. He wasn't, and I never heard from him again. He tossed me to the wayside after he took my virginity and using my name to influence directors across the industry to land him major roles. Karma was on my side though, because he was arrested for drug possession and solicitation of a prostitute not too long after. Of course, he never spent any time in jail and is just as notorious now as a bad boy than as a decent actor.

Ten minutes later, we pull up to the bar on the outskirts of the small downtown area. Sidewinders is lit up like a beacon in the night, directing any and everyone to its establishment. My eyes widen as I take in the line forming out the door, a muscled bouncer standing against the wall checking IDs and patting people down.

"Izzy, I don't think we're getting in anytime soon. That line is ridiculous."

What a waste of makeup.

She flips down the visor and applies some lip gloss in the mirror on the opposite side.

"Don't worry, that's just Sam. He's friends with Trevor. We'll get in."

I take another glance at the line wrapping around the bar and sigh. Maybe I'm not as up for this as I thought.

"I don't know about this."

"Come on, Quinn. You're a fucking movie star. You've been on red carpets with some of the most famous people on the planet. Hell, you *are* one of the most famous people on this planet. Don't tell me you're afraid of a few country boys."

"It's not the boys," I whisper. And it isn't. It's always the girls. The girls who liked to pick on me for being in drama club, who liked to make fun of the girl with a few extra pounds, who liked to shove their sexual escapades with Trevor in my face. Those girls knew how to make my life a living hell as a teenager, and I don't suspect that they've learned any better as an adult.

"It'll be fine, Quinn. You'll see. Let's go." She slides out from the vehicle, leaving me alone with my reservations.

Taking a deep breath, I murmur, "Here goes nothing," and follow her path.

As promised, we're immediately let into the bar, much to the dismay of the people waiting outside. I do my best to hide my face by looking at the ground, but I definitely recognize the look of shock when Sam scans my identification. I probably could've used a fake one, but I was home and I intended on being myself. I immediately snatch it from his grasp when he nods me inside, then make my way to the back of the bar, not paying attention to anyone around me.

Luckily I bump into Izzy once I reach the elongated wooden countertop along the back of the expansive room.

She orders us two margaritas, and with my nerves, I don't have the heart to tell her that I haven't had an ounce of alcohol since that fateful night after graduation. Once our drinks are served, I take a sip and turn my back to the bar to take in the space. Booths line the side, a few pool tables reside in a room off to the left, and directly in front of me are couples grinding against each other to the music. It sort of reminds me of the scene in *Dirty Dancing* when Baby carries the watermelon into the employee lounge and meets Johnny for the first time. Baby was mesmerized by the dancing.

Well, she may not have been, but as a young girl, I certainly was.

I feel a nudge to my ribs and look over at Izzy as she points at her drink. "Do you want another?"

My eyes shift down to the ice-filled glass in my hands and I'm surprised to find it empty.

"Sure, but I'll get these. Do you want another? Wait, how are we getting home?"

"Uber." At my confused glance, she continues, "We may be a small town, but we're not in the dark. Sam and a few of Trevor's friends are Uber drivers."

"Oh. Really?" I ask, remembering the rough group of guys Trevor used to hang with.

"Yep."

I shrug and place the order with the bartender, whose eyes scan me over a few times, trying to place me but coming up empty. Thank goodness. He hands us our drinks a moment later, and we turn back around to watch the crowd. The song on the jukebox in the corner changes, and Izzy's face lights up in delight.

"Oh my gosh, I love this! Come on, Quinn, we need to go dance."

She doesn't give me a second to decide, her thin fingers gripping my wrist tightly and pulling me behind her onto the makeshift dance floor. The crowd parts for us, mainly because Izzy pushes and shoves her way into the center.

Before I know it, we're dancing wildly in the center of the floor, no one around paying us any mind as we gyrate against one another.

"Whew, that was fun. I need another drink," Izzy says after two more songs play. She stalks off toward the bar, leaving me in the crowd.

I try to follow, but suddenly I'm pulled back against a hard chest that rocks his erection into my backside.

"My my, Quinn Miller. You sure have grown up."

My movements still as his hand snakes around the exposed skin of my waist.

"Don't touch me," I seethe. I try to jerk away but his grip holds firm.

"Come on. We've all seen you wearing less in those magazines. Did you come back to try a real man on for size?"

The fury builds inside me. This is exactly what I expected to happen. People would assume things about me because of my career, because of following my dreams.

In a flash, I rock my head backward and slam my skull against his nose, hearing the satisfying crunch of the cartilage instantly. His arm drops from my waist and I rush away through the crowd, the shouts and cries not deterring me.

"You were always such a bitch," the man yells out.

I make no move to turn around and find out who it is, but I know it's someone I went to school with.

"I'll take a shot of tequila, please," I beg from the bartender.

"Quinn, are you okay? Is that a good idea?"

"I have no idea, Izzy," I reply as I toss back the shot and then tap the minuscule glass for a second. "Just keep them coming," I demand.

The bartender eyes me speculatively and then shoots a glance to Izzy, who's pulled out her phone and is gesturing wildly with her arms while she speaks.

My mind begins to fuzz from the alcohol, and I welcome the blurriness. I welcome the fog blocking the unsettling memories that seem to have flooded my mind the moment I stepped back into Dale City.

The four shots of tequila loosen me up, and I soon find myself back in the crowd, paying no mind to the hands that try to grip and possess me. Instead, I'm lost in a world of my own, where I imagine the man of my dreams pressing himself against me as we sway to the music. Telling me how much he wants me, how much he has always wanted me. I let myself go and relax for the first time in years, picturing the green eyes that stole my heart as a young girl.

The hands pull away suddenly, but I don't stop moving to the beat of the music. My arms hold my glass above my body as my hips sway back and forth.

"Come on, sweetheart. Let's get you home."

My mind registers the deep and seductive voice as it caresses the back of my neck. Gooseflesh erupts along my skin, and I immediately halt my gyrations. I recognize the voice and the sensations it's always given me.

I turn around slowly, anticipating the first time I've seen him in years. And there he stands—blue shirt, blue pants, and golden badge.

Wait, what? Badge?

Oh fuck.

The bad boy of Dale City is now… a cop? And a sexy-as-sin one, as well. So, the troublemaker has reformed his ways to serve the common good. And I am royally screwed, because if there's one thing that tickles my fancy more than a bad boy, it's a man in uniform.

"Uh, hello there, Officer," I stammer as I register his hands on my arms, moving me toward the exit with Izzy following closely behind.

"I'm here to take you home."

"Am I in trouble?" I ask as I stumble out the door and onto the gravel. Before I crash into the rough asphalt, a strong arm wraps around my waist and pulls me back against his taut chest. My breath comes out in a whoosh at the movement, and then a gurgling sound rumbles in my stomach.

"Oh fuck. I'm going to be sick," I exclaim as I try to push away. I make it just far enough to vomit beside a car as I rest my arm on the hood.

"Are you sure you can handle her, Trevor? I knew I should've stopped her before the fourth shot."

"Four? Jesus Christ, Izzy, you should've stopped her at one."

"I know, but she seemed so lost. I was just trying to be a good friend."

I heave again after listening to their conversation and sigh once I feel like the rumbles have stopped. Standing up, I turn around but suddenly realize it was too quick. The world closes in, blackness surrounding me.

"Shit," Trevor shouts.

All I remember before I pass out is strong arms wrapping around me and the feeling of weightlessness.

CHAPTER THREE
Trevor

I SWAT AT THE alarm blaring on my nightstand. Five o'clock comes way too quickly when you didn't get in until after midnight. Knowing I need to get a workout in before I head to the office, I begrudgingly roll out of bed. Searching in the darkness, I pull on a pair of black basketball shorts, tug on a pair of socks, and lace my running shoes.

Running has always been a way of clearing my head, and with all of the memories flooding into my mind, running is exactly what I need. Memories involving a woman who had once been the center of my everything.

Closing the door behind me, I step out of the house and make my way down the driveway toward the road. I try my best to keep my attention on the asphalt in front of me, but my eyes wander on their own accord to the small ranch across the street. The house where my sister and her best friend are residing.

"Stop it," I mutter as I force my attention from the house, wondering if Quinn is resting peacefully.

I hadn't imagined how good she would feel in my arms as her small body pressed against my chest when I carried her up the stairs. I was surprised when I approached the dance floor to find Quinn rotating her hips seductively to the music. Izzy's phone call had been frantic and concerned. I had immediately left my desk where I had been filling out the day's paperwork and made my way to Sidewinders, not expecting what I would find when I arrived. Quinn half naked and dancing as if her life depended on it was not on my spectrum.

For a moment I focused on her: her clear porcelain skin, the sinewy muscles of her legs and arms, and the deep cut of her shirt revealing the ample breasts I had daydreamed about since I was a teen. She hadn't just changed the way she had dressed; instead, she had gotten better with age.

Quinn had been a typical woman with a buzz—a little bit of slurring, unsteady on her feet, and a bit touchy-feely. She may not remember that her hand had brushed across my cock that had already been straining behind my pants, but my dick certainly did.

And with that thought, my cock begins to stiffen behind my shorts as I run, never a pleasant experience. I try my damnedest to think about anything else. Mrs. Englehart in her muumuu walking around town with half of the dress tucked in her adult underwear. Old Mr. Johnson buying a box of condoms at the pharmacy for his new ninety-year-old girlfriend.

There that did it. Thank God.

Five miles later, I jog my way back up the steps of my house. I feel the pull to turn my attention around, to get one last glance at Izzy's house, but I refrain. Instead, I slam my front door shut and head to my bathroom in desperate need of a shower.

The tension in my body subsides as I step under the hot spray. I reach for the soap and rub it against my heated skin, the suds dripping down my body in a parade of their own. I close my eyes and relax under the shower head, but instead of the blankness that I yearn to welcome, I'm blessed with visions of Quinn's lush body pressed against mine as I held her up when she passed out.

My cock grows, and I reach down and palm it gently, the erection jumping against my hold. I stroke it up and down as I recall how perfectly her ass fit against my hips, the cheeks cradling my member completely. The way the swell of her lush breasts rubbed against my forearm. The way my arm wrapped snuggly around her trim waist. The scent of her hair as it filled my nostrils.

What would it be like to take her? To feel her naked body pressed against mine? To slide my dick into her hot center?

I stroke myself faster, imagining all of the things I want to do to Quinn Miller. I'm startled as I erupt in my own palm, something I haven't done in years. There is never a shortage of women to finish the job for me. I feel like the same sixteen-year-old I was when Quinn was part of my life and we had been best friends. But when my fantasies about her became out of control, I knew I needed to step back or I'd hurt both her and my sister. The two most important people in my life.

Back in my room, I pull on my uniform and situate the gun on my hip. We don't have a lot of crime in Dale City, but with Quinn in town, I've made it my personal objective to keep her safe. Not that I had a choice. The chief of police assumed that, since my sister was her best friend, I would have the most opportunities to keep an eye on her. He wasn't wrong, but he wasn't right either. I had planned to do everything in my power to maintain my distance.

The second alarm on my phone buzzes and I check the time: 6:30 a.m. I snatch one final item off my dresser and head out of the house, crossing the street. With my spare key, I unlock Izzy's door. Listening closely, I search for any noise but hear none and hope the girls are still asleep. Knowing my sister is just like me, an early riser, I decide to start some breakfast in her kitchen. Not just for her, but because my house is empty of food and I'm starving.

Opening her fridge, I sigh with relief when I see she's stocked it recently. I snag some eggs, bacon, mushrooms, spinach, and cheese, the makings for some omelets.

I get to work at the stove making the first omelet when I hear bare footsteps enter the kitchen. I turn around, assuming it's Izzy, but choke on my own tongue when I find Quinn standing there in nothing but an oversized gray shirt barely covering the top of her thighs.

"Hey," she whispers. "I wasn't expecting to see anyone this early."

I continue to stare at her, not only because I'm surprised that she's awake at this hour, but because she looks just as breathtaking all mussed up with alcohol-fueled sleep as she does on the infamous magazine covers she graces.

I'm finally able to speak and I attempt to smile warmly at her, but it probably comes out as a grimace because Quinn's face scrunches in confusion.

"What are you doing here?" she asks.

"Well, I'm making breakfast before I head into the office."

She settles in a chair at the table but keeps her gaze on me, sending spikes of adrenaline through my body.

"Office? You work on a Saturday?"

Plating the first two omelets, I set one in front of her and then take the seat opposite.

"Sweetheart, I work pretty much every day."

"Every day?" She jabs her fork into the soft mixture of eggs and vegetables and takes a hearty bite. A moan escapes her lips as she tosses her head back in ecstasy.

Fuck, how good would it feel to be the one to cause her to moan like that?

"When did you learn to cook like this? I don't remember that growing up," Quinn asks as she takes another bite.

"I've always known how. Mom said I needed to know how to be self-sufficient."

"Well, I can testify that Izzy can't cook like this to save her life."

I laugh at her assessment, knowing she's right. Izzy can burn water.

"Mom gave up on her when she burned noodles in her favorite pot." Quinn grimaces as I continue, "And to answer your question, yes, I work pretty much every day. That's the life of a cop."

"Don't you take vacations?"

"Haven't been able to for a while."

She seems to think on that for a while as silence grows in the room. I watch as she finishes her breakfast and then stands to retrieve two glasses from the cupboard, grabs the orange juice from the fridge, and pours it into the two glasses. Quinn places one glass in front of me without a word.

"So tell me, how does a man known in Dale City as Trevor the Troublemaker become a cop?"

"Pretty simple, if you think about it. Who better to catch a troublemaker than another troublemaker?"

"Good point." She nods as she finishes her juice with a final gulp, leaving a drop on the edge of her plump lip. I watch as her pink tongue peeks out of the corner to catch the escapee and then back into her mouth.

Damn it, she's turning me on by just drinking juice.

"My turn. How does it feel to get everything you've ever dreamed of?"

Her eyes widen in surprise, obviously not expecting the question. Luckily for her, Izzy walks in before she has a chance to respond.

"Good morning," Izzy rejoices as she steps over to the stove and snags the last omelet resting on the warming plate.

"Hey, Iz."

"I'm surprised to see you up, Quinn. And not hungover either. Impressive."

"Should I be? I don't really remember much from last night," Quinn admits with a slight blush on her cheeks.

Before Izzy has a chance to speak up, I say, "Well, you had four shots of tequila after a couple of margaritas and made Sidewinders your own personal dance stage last night. When we left the bar, you vomited all over the side of Wendy Smithson's car and then promptly passed out. I carried you back to Izzy's house and put you to bed."

Her eyes widen with each word until they're as round as saucers.

Whispering, she asks, "Who changed me?" as she looks down at the shirt barely covering her.

I wink in her direction. "Izzy did, sweetheart. Don't worry."

"I'm sorry I caused such a ruckus. That man put his hands on me and I just snapped. No one seems to understand personal space anymore."

"What man?" Izzy and I exclaim simultaneously.

"Just some guy from high school that took his dancing just a bit too far. I wasn't prepared. Usually my security doesn't let anyone within a ten-foot radius of me."

"I'll repeat, what man?" My body seethes at the thought of someone we know putting his hands on her as if she is property.

"Devin Shomaker. He was a grade above us, I believe. Please don't do anything, Trevor. I just want to forget about it and enjoy the rest of my time here."

Sympathy and understanding surge through me, but I will need to check in with Devin before I can let this go. I can't imagine what it's like to have to constantly fight a battle for privacy. This must be part of the reason she decided to come home finally.

"It's fine, Quinn. We're all allowed to break free every once in a while," Izzy assures as she sits down with her plate.

"Well, ladies, I'm headed to work. I'm assuming I'll see you both for dinner tonight?"

"Dinner?" Quinn's blonde hair moves as she cocks her head.

"Yes, my parents still hold Friday family dinners, but they've moved this one to Saturday to accommodate your arrival. You know they'll be upset if you don't come."

"You know I wouldn't miss it. I love your family."

I lean down to press a kiss on Izzy's cheek and then do the same to Quinn, reveling in the feel of her soft skin beneath my lips.

"See y'all tonight."

I head back across the street with my heart pounding. I knew I was attracted to Quinn—hell, most every man on the planet is attracted to her—but I never anticipated the spark of awareness when she was around, the pulse of electricity through my veins at her touch. It would be too much for someone else, but I spent the better part of my adolescence maintaining control where Quinn was concerned.

How hard could one more month be?

Once I arrive at my office, my cell phone vibrates in my pocket and "Mom" flashes across the screen.

"Well, to what do I owe this pleasure?" I declare into the receiver.

Mom chuckles and then tsks at me. "Is it not okay for me to call my favorite son?"

"Only son. And on a Saturday, it's usually when you need something."

"That is not true!" she exclaims.

"Mom…," I draw out, waiting for her to explain her reasoning for calling at eight on a Saturday morning when she very well knows I'm in the office.

"Fine. I ordered Quinn's favorite dessert from the bakery. Could you pick it up on your way over?"

"Boston crème pie?"

I hadn't indulged in a slice of that pie in ages, the taste reminding me of my own favorite morsel. When she left Dale City, so did my desire for anything that reminded me of her.

"That's it. I'm so excited to see her. It's been far too long."

"Mom, you saw her on a video chat with Izzy like three weeks ago."

"Boy, don't sass me. You know that isn't the same thing as having her back home. I don't know what changed between you two, but you were always the best of friends. You should take some time off to catch up."

"People grow up, Mom. And you know I'm busy right now since we're down two officers."

"Excuses. Well, maybe she'll meet a nice boy while she's here and move back home. Wouldn't that be nice?"

Nice? It would be fucking torture to see her prance around town with someone else.

"Yeah, nice, Mom. Look, I need to finish up this paperwork so I can head out on time. Do you need anything else?"

"Just the pie. We'll see you at six."

Hanging up, I rest back in my chair, sighing. I'm the only one here today, the only one without a family to spend my weekends with, and that's how I wanted it. Closing my eyes, I imagine how I would feel if Quinn moved back to Dale City, if I would be able to tolerate seeing her with another man.

In high school, it was never an issue, Quinn had her heart and soul focused on the drama club and the theater group she participated in while I had been the one with different girlfriends every week. My crush on Quinn was a closely guarded secret that I planned on taking to the grave.

Before I know it, the clock shows it's well past lunchtime. Setting the files on the chief's desk, I drive toward the bakery to pick up the pie for Quinn, then head back to my house.

Normally I would go straight to my parents' house in my uniform, but tonight, for some reason, I want to show Quinn what I've become. What she's missed out on in the six years since we lost contact. I'm feeling spiteful after imagining her with someone else all morning. I knew she had crushed on me growing up. It was part of the reason why I needed to stay away from her as a teen, because I knew if she gave me an inch, I would've taken a mile. And a mile of Quinn Miller was never going to be enough.

I tug on a fitted gray shirt that I've been told on numerous occasions shows off my muscles and a pair of jeans that hug my thighs. My workouts were intense, and I got gratification from the ripped muscles I sported.

With one final look in the mirror, I grab the pie off the counter and get in the car. My parents only live about five minutes away, and when I pull into the driveway, I see my sister and Quinn have already arrived.

Once in the house, I move toward the kitchen but the door to the powder room swings open, knocking the boxed pie into my chest.

Quinn's brown eyes widen in surprise and then despair as she takes in the box squished against my chest, now dripping some of its contents.

"Trevor, I'm so sorry."

Seeing how upset she is, I unleash one of my signature smirks and watch as the redness rises in her cheeks.

Leaning close to her ear, box still cradled against my chest, I whisper, "Don't worry, Quinn. I've always wanted to smear your cream all over me."

The gasp that sounds at my retreat is all I need to know that Ms. Movie Star isn't as completely unaffected by me as she seems.

RENEE HARLESS

CHAPTER FOUR
Quinn

O H MY GOSH. OH *my gosh. Oh my gosh,* I chant in my head as I watch Trevor's retreating back. A well-muscled retreating back.

I thought my feelings for him would've receded with time and distance, but that obviously isn't the case. Everything seems ten times more heightened since I saw him in the kitchen this morning. My heart didn't stop pounding for almost an hour after he left, like the crazed thirteen-year-old I used to be.

And if what he whispered in my ear is any indication, then he knows how I used to feel about him, and may have even reciprocated those feelings.

Izzy bumps into me in the hallway. "Your face is all flushed. Are you feeling okay?"

"Yes, it… um… must be the heat. I'm still adjusting to the humidity."

She must buy my tale because she skirts past me into the kitchen, where I quickly follow. As we enter, I hear the bit of conversation between Trevor and his mom.

"I'm sorry, Mom. I tripped coming in the house."

Is he taking the blame? I'm the one who slammed into him leaving the bathroom.

"Well, shoot. That's okay, honey."

"Did you want me to run out and grab another? I can even get a police escort. It is an emergency, after all."

Mrs. Shaw's light chuckle joins my own.

"You don't need to do that. I just wanted Quinn's welcome home to be a special one."

And if my heart wasn't already beating wildly, it is now. His mother has always treated me better than my own, and the fact that she wants to make my short visit special speaks volumes about the wonderful woman she is.

"Why don't you grab a clean shirt from the laundry room? I'm sure I still have a few."

I try to move, but not quickly enough because I come face-to-face with an exiting Trevor as he removes his shirt. I struggle to catch my breath as I watch each of his muscles bend and flex when he lifts the cotton over his head and releases his arms back to his side.

Wow, Trevor Shaw has grown into quite a man. He had always been a bit more developed than the other boys in high school, but this takes it to a whole new level. He doesn't have an ounce of fat on his body. I've been around some of the men who are considered the most beautiful in the world, but they don't hold a candle to Trevor.

Suddenly he walks up to me and crosses his arms.

"Like what you see, sweetheart?"

I swallow loudly, but no words come. For some reason, my comprehension flies out the window whenever Trevor tries to speak to me.

He smirks. "I'll be right back. Have to go change my shirt."

"Uh-huh. I'll… um… save you a seat."

He chuckles as he walks past me, his arm rubbing against my own, and I have to fight the urge to run my hand up his muscled chest.

And then I think about what I said. *"Save you a seat?" It's his parents' freaking home. I'm an idiot.*

With my nerves at an all-time high, I rush through the kitchen into the formal dining room and take the seat that was always reserved for me during my visits while in school.

"Thank you for inviting me, Mrs. Shaw."

"Now don't you start that again. It took me three years to break that habit the first time. My name is Sue, and I expect you to call me by that name."

"Yes, ma'am."

"Now everyone load their plates. Tonight we're having Quinn's favorite. Welcome home, honey."

"Pot roast?"

"Yes, and all the fixings."

My mouth instantly waters, and I don't have to be told twice. I dive into the serving dish in front of me and load my plate full of roast, potatoes, and vegetables.

It all looks amazing, but it doesn't compare to the man who saunters into the dining room, black shirt now encasing his chest. His hair looks damp, as if he's wet his hands and run them through the strands. He strolls closer toward me and I practically choke on the carrot I just placed in my mouth. I have to cough a few times to dislodge the offensive vegetable as he takes the open seat next to me. Something I had failed to notice.

"You okay, sweetheart?" he asks.

I nod furiously and decide that the best plan of action to get through this dinner is to keep feeding myself as much food as possible. I barely take a breath as I finish my plate in rapid speed.

A hand brushes against my bare legs below my skirt's hem.

"What are you doing?" I whisper-shout as Trevor bends down, his knuckles trailing down my calf, and then repeats the movement as he rises.

"Sorry, I dropped my napkin," he explains as he situates the cloth on his lap.

Before I can say any more, he winks at me and then starts eating.

"This dinner's lovely, Mrs.... I mean Sue."

"Thank you, dear. It's so wonderful to have you home. Have you given any thought to moving back permanently? I know Izzy would love to have you close by once again."

My heart starts racing for a different reason. I hate letting people down, but my life is in LA. My career and my friends—well, the few I have.

Few? Ha. The one friend I have.

"Well, I, um...."

"Mom, don't go putting her on the spot. She has a great career, and living in LA makes it easier, I'm sure. Give her a break," Trevor chimes in, and I glance over my shoulder at him in awe.

I had expected for their mom and Izzy to push the issue until I promised more visits, something to appease them, but he shut them down without a thought.

"Thank you," I mouth, and he replies with a nod.

"Tell us what you plan to do while you're here," Jake, Izzy and Trevor's father, inquires.

"Well, I have a script to work on. It's a romantic comedy, so it's a bit different than the dramatic roles I've done in the past. Actually, do you all know if Mr. Timmons still runs the drama department at the high school?"

A clanking noise interrupts my thoughts, and I watch as Trevor's fork clinks against the plate, following his knife. He glares daggers at his sister.

"You didn't tell her?"

"Tell me what?"

Izzy wipes her mouth with her napkin. "I'm sorry. You told me not to mention anything about home."

"I don't understand. What's going on?"

"The entire Arts department at the high school was shut down due to budget cuts about four years ago. Mr. Timmons moved to Georgia with his wife not long after," Trevor explains.

"So there is no drama department in Dale City?"

He shakes his head and my heart drops. I never imagined that they would cut the program from the schools. It always had a large group of dedicated students, and when I attended, we raised all of our own funds.

"What about the community theater?"

"That's gone too. When Mr. Timmons left, there was no one who wanted to head it up. I'm sorry, Quinn,"

Sue shares in a voice meant to soothe me, but it does the opposite.

The chair creaks as I push away from the table and excuse myself. I blindly navigate the hallway and head toward the sunroom through the tears building in my eyes. I can't believe the drama department and theater group are gone. They were the only things that gave me hope when I was growing up. It's how I realized the one thing I wanted to do with my life. Without them, I don't know what would've happened to me. They were my escape from the home where my parents were rarely around or paid me little attention. There was a roof over my head and food on the table, but no love.

Finally in the sunroom, I rest my head against the glass overlooking the flower garden in Sue's backyard. I take a few deep breaths, something I was taught to help calm my nerves, but it doesn't seem to work. The pain of knowing that something I used to hold dear has now been stripped away is almost too much to bear.

"I thought I'd find you here," a deep, gravelly voice announces.

I don't need to turn around to know it's Trevor. I actually felt him before he spoke. My body always seems to know when he's near.

"This was always your favorite spot in the house. I remember that now."

Maintaining my gaze out the window, I ask him, "Why would they keep this from me?" Gazing over my shoulder, I look into his sympathetic eyes and continue. "They knew how important those programs were to me. I could've helped. I could've saved them." I end on a sob and let the tears fall.

Suddenly I find myself encased by two strong arms, my face pressed against Trevor's chest. Even amidst the turmoil soaring through me, my body still reacts to his closeness, my own arms going around his waist as I pull him tighter.

"I'm sorry, Quinn. In hindsight, I'm sure Izzy and Mom thought they were doing what you requested."

Trevor allows me to cry, let out the pain of knowing my favorite teacher is gone, along with the root of my passion.

Once my cries slow, he caresses my back and neck before coming to rest at my jawline. My head tilts back on its own, and I gaze up into Trevor's concerned green eyes.

"Better?" he asks.

"As better as I can be, I suppose."

With a bob of his head, his thumbs begin to caress the soft skin along my jaw. "I'm sorry, sweetheart."

"Why do you call me that?" I whisper, losing myself in his touch. He doesn't respond, but his pulse increases. "Trevor?"

Again he doesn't respond, but the air between us crackles violently. He leans forward, and I brace myself for the kiss I've been anticipating since I was thirteen. My eyes close and I hold my breath as I wait to feel his lips against my own. But I'm disappointed when his mouth brushes my forehead instead.

Embarrassed, my eyes shoot open as he retreats from my grasp.

"What's going on in here?" Izzy blurts as she strolls into the room.

"N-nothing, Iz. Trevor just came to calm me down, that's all."

My eyes follow as he leaves the room without a backward glance toward me.

"It looked like more than that. I mean, how weird would that be. I can't imagine you and Trevor together."

"Why would that be weird?" Her eyes narrow and I quickly add, "Just out of curiosity."

"Because we're all like siblings. It would be strange. Plus you're my friend, and he sleeps with more woman than I can count. He would only hurt you, Quinn."

"Oh I know. I was just wondering."

Izzy takes my hand and guides me back to the dining room while she apologizes for not telling me about Mr. Timmons. As we pass the kitchen, I watch as Trevor tosses back a glass of amber liquid before meeting my eyes. I try to hold his stare, but he quickly looks over to the dining room where his mother's setting out a pie.

"It's no Boston crème, but I think apple will do."

I smile. "It looks delicious."

As we sit down for dessert and coffee, I explain to Jake the synopsis of the script I'm reading about a second-chance romance. He seems riveted, so I continue explaining the characters and the scenes.

"I have it!" Sue shouts.

"Have what?" Trevor asks.

"Oh, right. I know who can do the read-through with you. Trevor can do it. He has years of built-up vacation time, so I doubt his boss would mind if he took time off."

Izzy's and Trevor's faces pale in alarm. "We're short-staffed at the office. I can't just request time off, Mom. And on top of that, what the hell do I know about reading a script?"

"Oh, you just have to read the lines and maybe act out a few scenes. Quinn is a professional. She just needs you to stand in," Sue explains. My palms begin to sweat and I rub them against my skirt as my anxiety builds.

"I don't want Trevor to use his vacation time to help me." Plus I'm afraid I won't be able to control myself around him if we're put together for long periods of time. "I'm sure there are a few of my old drama friends still living close by. I could probably call them up."

"Fine, but I still think it's a good idea. It's not like he lives far away."

"What do you mean?"

"I own the house across the street," he offers.

Well damn. I didn't realize how close the proximity truly was. *I'm really going to have to control myself now.*

I force a laugh at the situation, and luckily Jake and Sue change the topic to Izzy's new employee at the bank. The coffee burns as I gulp it down, but I welcome the pain, anything to take my mind off running lines with Trevor. If anyone could break me from encompassing the role, it would be him.

I take another large gulp of the scorching liquid, knowing I'll regret the burnt feeling in my mouth tomorrow, and glance over the rim of my mug at Trevor.

His paleness replaced by a cocky smile, as if he can read my thoughts, he winks and then licks his lips.

That bastard knows I was imagining losing control with him if we practiced the script.

Another mark in Trevor's column. In the short span of four hours, he's spun my head about three times too many.

How am I going to survive the rest of the month?

RENEE HARLESS

CHAPTER FIVE
Quinn

"SO, WHAT ARE WE looking for exactly?" Izzy asks as I steer the cart down another grocery aisle. Shopping has been a luxury I haven't had the chance to enjoy in a long time; I'm usually bombarded by fans or paparazzi, and I never get the chance to grab the items I need. Thank goodness for online shopping where the local market will just deliver them to my door. It saves me the hassle of having to deal with photographers and overly eager fans.

"I don't know, really. I don't want to eat your things." I snag a bag of cookies off the shelf.

"Guess we're going the junk food route."

Laughing, I nod. "You know it. Now let's head to the ice cream. I feel some rocky road in my future."

I notice a group of people trailing behind us with their own buggies and my nerves set in.

"Izzy, are those people following us?"

She turns her head and narrows her eyes at the crowd before picking up her pace.

"Yes, and they have cameras too. I'm sorry, Quinn."

"That's okay. I should've known better. Let's grab the last few things, and then we can check out."

After another ten minutes, the crowd grows to an incredible size, making it impossible for Izzy and me to exit the aisle.

"What do we do?" she asks me frantically.

I do my best to remain calm, but as they push closer, my anxiety rises. We stand behind our carts, blocking them from coming any farther.

The store manager tries to push his way through the crowd but he's unsuccessful, further squashing my hopes of getting out anytime soon.

"I think we're just going to have to wait it out," I sigh remembering how awful it felt the first time that this occurred in LA. The moment was terrifying and it's why security never lets me shop alone. "Hopefully the manager will call the police."

"I've already sent a text to Trevor. They're on their way."

Good. Hopefully he and Izzy will get a glimpse of what my life is like. Why I never wanted to bring this to their doorstep. Fame has a vicious downside, and I refuse to bring that to the two people closest to me.

The crowd's voices grow in earnest, questions spewing from their mouths in a voracious spiral.

"Quinn, did you get fired?"

"Did you hear Alex was caught kissing that supermodel? Is that why you're hiding?"

"Are you moving back?"

"Are you expecting an Academy nomination this year?"

My head spins as the questions continue to swirl around me. It seems people in my hometown are mini-paparazzi of their own.

Izzy and I cower into ourselves as more people join the crowd.

"I'm so sorry, Izzy. I didn't expect this to happen."

She reaches down and grabs my hand, squeezing it gently. "They're just curious, that's all. It'll die down."

Leave it to Izzy to turn a horrible situation into a learning moment.

A deep voice roars over the crowd as the sound of sirens echoes in the parking lot. "Get back!"

I sigh with relief. *We're finally being rescued.*

"Move!" Trevor shouts again until finally he breaks through the crowd, his eyes wild with concern and distress. "Are you both okay? Are you hurt?"

We shake our heads as he steps through our makeshift barrier and takes us in. He checks over his sister first, a gesture that hurts far more than it should, and then he turns to me.

Cupping my chin, he tilts my head back, worry filling his gaze. "You have tears in your eyes."

"It was just a lot, that's all. I'm more worried about Izzy than myself."

"I'm so sorry, sweetheart. Let's get you home."

Glancing down at my cart one more time, I see the ice cream dripping.

"I don't think my dessert is going to make it."

Trevor chuckles, one of my favorite sounds, then wraps his arm protectively around my shoulders as Izzy sidles up to him.

"Don't worry, I'm pretty sure I have some back at my place."

"Your place?" I ask as he veers us through the crowd, each person still vying for their perfect shot of me. And now I worry that a picture of me, Trevor, and Izzy will be plastered in the latest gossip magazine, pegging us in a love triangle.

"Yep, I figured I could treat you both tonight. What do you say to pizza?"

He looks down at me and I notice a flash of hope in his irises.

"Pizza sounds great, actually."

*

INSTEAD OF A RANCH style like the house Izzy lives in, Trevor lives in a quaint craftsman across the street. Truthfully, it's probably my favorite house on the block. And the interior isn't as masculine as I had imagined. Instead, it's warm and inviting, a complete one-eighty from the man shoving his fifth slice of pizza into his delectable mouth.

"Do you guys want to watch a movie?" Izzy asks from her perch on the floor between Trevor's and my legs.

"Sure," I reply as I snatch a pepperoni from my pizza slice. I could swear I heard a groan coming from Trevor's direction, but when I peek over his way, I find his attention is on the blank screen of the television.

"*Ghostbusters*?"

"Which one?" I ask with a full mouth.

"The second. Come on, Quinn. You know I love the Titanic part."

Reaching forward, I grab my can of Dr. Pepper and take a sip as I giggle at Izzy's proclamation. The second has always been her favorite. Mine too, but Trevor only likes the first one, and he despised when we would rule him out as kids.

"Well, I'm not the one you have to convince." I nod toward a scowling Trevor.

Izzy begins to go into all of the reasons why the second film trumps the first, so I take the now-empty pizza box and the few cans of soda into the kitchen, tossing everything in the trash before heading to the sink to wash my hands.

The familiar prickles rise on my arms, and then his masculine sandalwood scent carries across my nose. My hands automatically freeze under the warm water pouring from the faucet. Trevor presses his body against mine, and I suck in a breath. I wish I wasn't so affected by him. I practically shiver as his hands glide down my arms to rest under the water with mine. My eyes close as his nose brushes along my jaw. I don't even notice when he reaches for the soap and begins to suds up our hands together. His fingers slide between each of mine as he continues to increase the lather, and his lips press against the sensitive skin below my ear.

My breath hitches at the contact, which seems to break him from the erotic foreplay he unleashed on me. I never knew handwashing could be such a turn-on. He reaches up to turn off the faucet and then grabs the dish towel. I just stand there frozen, unable to do anything but let my hands drip-dry in the sink.

"Better to share than letting the water go to waste," he explains with a sexy smirk, the corner of his mouth tilting upward.

I watch his backside as he leisurely walks back to the living room.

Dammit, this round goes to Trevor again. At this point, I'm about to start losing count.

"Quinn, are you coming?" Izzy shouts from the den, and I hurriedly dry my hands.

"Sorry, I was checking to see if there's any popcorn," I lie, narrowing my eyes as Trevor coughs behind his hand. It's then that I notice that Izzy has taken up residence on the couch beside Trevor. The only available seat is on Trevor's other side.

This will be okay. You've sat beside him dozens of times.

As the movie starts, Izzy requests the lights be shut off, so I flick the switch on the way to the couch. I sit as far away from Trevor as possible, pretty much resting my body on the arm of the sofa. It's uncomfortable, but not as uncomfortable as it would be for me to sit with my body pressed against Trevor's.

The movie starts and we settle in to watch, but about fifteen minutes in, I begin to squirm from the awkwardness of my position. I bring my legs up onto the couch only to have my ankle grabbed. My head swings to

Trevor, who has his attention pinned to the movie. I try to pull my ankle away but his grip tightens.

"What are you doing?" I whisper, trying not to draw Izzy's attention.

Trevor doesn't answer right away; instead, he turns his head and pins me with his gaze. I'm immobilized by his stare and begin to question if I indeed find lust in his eyes. Lust that definitely matches what's firing in mine.

"Come here," he mouths as he tugs on my ankle once more.

"No," I mouth back.

Then he unleashes his secret weapon, his lower lip puckering out and his eyebrows rising upward in a practiced puppy dog face.

"Please," he requests, and I give in to the pull.

I settle in next to Trevor but remain stiff until he reaches across the back of the couch and rests his hand on my shoulder. His fingers begin to trace lazy circles on the exposed skin from my tank top, and my shoulders relax.

We watch the remainder of the movie like this, his fingers tracing an invisible pattern on my shoulder and my hands tucked firmly under my crossed arms so I don't give in to the urge to touch him.

I'm so lost in the movements that I don't even notice when the movie ends. It takes Izzy standing from the couch and flicking on the light switch before I edge away from Trevor and let his arm drop between the couch and my back. His fingers take charge and edge past my top, stroking the skin at my waist. I jump up in fear of Izzy seeing.

"You ready to go, Quinn?" she asks. "I have to work in the morning."

"Sure. Thanks for saving us today, Trevor."

He remains sitting on the couch, cocky mug firmly in place. "It was my pleasure, Quinn." He winks up at me.

I move away from the couch and the powerful pull Trevor has over me and follow Izzy out of the house and across the street.

"I meant to ask if you had any luck with finding someone to help you with your script."

As she unlocks the front door, I follow her inside and explain, "Unfortunately no. Everyone kept pushing me to call someone else. I mean, it's not like I'm asking for a kidney, just a few days a week to read through the lines. Is that so much to ask?"

"I'm sorry. You'll find someone."

"At this point I'm about to ask your mom. She's free at night, right?"

"Good luck convincing my dad of that."

"Damn. This shouldn't be so difficult."

Izzy shrugs sympathetically and then wishes me good night.

I stalk to my bedroom and tug on an oversized shirt and gym shorts before grabbing the script from the dresser. I try a few scenes, but I've never been one to complete a read-through without someone to act out the other characters, needing to feed off their energy and words.

"Ugh!" I grumble into the empty room and flop back onto the bed.

This trip back home is not going as planned. First, I'm not able to focus on the script like I wanted. Second, my parents got wind that I'm home and are requesting my presence for some unknown reason. And finally, Trevor has ignited my carefully guarded crush from childhood and it's exploded into full-blown infatuation.

Closing my eyes, I can't help but remember how it felt tonight in his kitchen when he pressed me against the sink and cradled my body to his. A shiver rattles down my body recalling the way his hands felt on my arms.

I don't think my attraction to him is one-sided this time around, and that scares the daylights out of me. Because if we give in to the attraction, neither of us is going to win.

Turning my head, I stare at the script, yearning for it to speak to me, to give me an idea of who I can call, but only one idea settles in my mind.

Sliding on my flip-flops, I quietly open the front door and skip out into the night. A light's on in the upper bedroom of Trevor's house, and I pray he hasn't gone to bed.

Like a thief in the night, I stalk up to his house and try the doorknob—locked. I take a deep breath and try to calm my nerves before I knock on the door. I can hear his heavy footsteps as he travels down the stairs, and I stare at him in awe as he opens the door.

Once again, I'm met with the naked chest of Trevor Shaw. I take my time to scan him completely, because... well, because I can. His gray sweatpants hang low on his hips, dangerously low. A light smattering of hair trails down from his navel to the top of the pants, directing the eye to what can only be described as an impressive piece of manhood. I swallow a gasp and continue my observation as I count the eight extended muscles in his abdomen. *Are those nipple rings? How did I miss those last time?* He bears no visible tattoos, but the nipple rings give him that bad boy appearance he wore like a badge of honor as a teen.

"If you keep staring at me like that, I'll be forced to toss you over my shoulder and show you what I can do with these muscles."

My mouth hangs open in surprise, and he reaches out and moves my chin upward, effectively closing my mouth.

"Did you need something, Quinn?"

"No... I mean yes. Do you think... I mean, you can say no, but what I'm trying to ask—"

"Quinn," he barks.

"Sorry, do you think you can help me with the script read? I can't find anyone else who's willing. We can do it when you're off work or whenever works for you. I'll be at your beck and call."

He takes a moment to consider my request before a conniving smile graces his lips. "My beck and call, you say?"

I try not to read into the hidden meaning of his words as I agree.

"You have a deal, sweetheart."

Thrilled, I launch myself at him, wrapping my arms around his neck and my legs around his waist. I don't notice how he stiffens or how good he feels in my arms; I do note how one of his hands comes to rest on my ass and the other snakes around my waist.

We stay like this for a moment, but unfortunately my grip begins to loosen and I slide down his body. I have to hold back my gasp as his erection grazes against my stomach, but his growl doesn't go unnoticed.

"I'm sorry, I got a bit carried away. So... I'll see you tomorrow? Or not? I mean... just text me when you're available. Izzy or your mom can give you my number."

I spin on my heels and jog down the steps without so much as a goodbye, embarrassment reddening my cheeks.

"Hey, Quinn!" Trevor shouts into the dark night air, and I turn around as I reach the end of his walkway. "I'll see you tomorrow at six."

I nod in acknowledgment and make my way back to Izzy's house, praying I haven't made a colossal mistake.

RENEE HARLESS

CHAPTER SIX
Trevor

HE SOY SAUCE MIXTURE bubbles in the pan as I pour it over the chicken and vegetables. Quinn hadn't suggested dinner, but I figured she could always snack while I ate.

Her request last night hadn't taken me by surprise, I figured most of her old colleagues would freak out over working with her. What had surprised me was her response to my agreement. When her legs had wrapped around my waist, I had to do everything possible to keep from bringing her inside my house and having my way with her.

It wasn't just that her body was perfection—lush curves, small waist, smooth skin. Her personality reminds me of the innocent little girl who moved across the street from me as a teenager. Her fragile goodness beckons me, and it's taking practiced restraint to hold back.

And yet here I am inviting her to do the read-through in my house.

"I should've suggested the library," I murmur, then remember how sexy she looked playing a librarian in the film she released last year. I'd drag her off to the antique stacks in the basement.

The buzzer for the rice sounds in the kitchen at the same time there's a knock at the door.

Fuck, she's here.

I turn off the gas to the stove before I make my way to the door. In the mirror in the hall, I check my face one quick time, then glance down at my black T-shirt and camouflage cargo shorts. Satisfied with my appearance, I open the door and openly moan at the sight before me.

Quinn's blonde hair is curled at the ends and pushed over one shoulder, showcasing her small ear where a sparkling jewel greets me. The soft peach dress hugs her chest and skims down her waist to flare out and stop at her upper thighs. My eyes never waver from that point, stuck on the smooth, milky skin at the top of her thighs.

A cough interrupts my musing, and I glance up at Quinn to find her bashfully smiling.

"Hi, Trevor."

"Quinn, please come in. I wasn't sure if you'd eaten, but I have some stir fry ready to go," I offer, leading her to the kitchen. Even without turning around, I can feel her eyes boring into my backside, and I mentally fist-pump.

"This smells amazing." She inhales deeply as her eyes shut.

"Can I make you a plate?"

"Mmm, yes, please."

At the kitchen table, she pulls out a chair and sits down casually, placing the stack of white papers on the tabletop. My tongue practically wags out of my mouth when her skirt rides higher on her thighs.

I fill a couple ceramic plates and set them on the table.

"Bon appétit."

"Thanks, Trevor. This looks great." With her fork full of vegetables and chicken, she places it in her mouth and moans in delight. "So good."

"Thank you."

Finally scooping some of the food in my mouth, I enjoy the comfortable silence of our meal.

"So tell me, how does this new and improved Trevor Shaw come from the same Trevor who evoked fear in most of our teachers?" she asks curiously.

"Well, looks can be deceiving. I never did any of the things I was accused of."

"Not even gluing the principal to his seat?"

"Not even that one."

"So why did you take the blame?"

"It was just easier than fighting the system. I knew I hadn't done anything, and so did my parents. That's all that mattered to me."

"Wow, I feel like I never knew you at all."

"Well, just because I wasn't the one who did them doesn't mean I wasn't there when it happened. I just made sure to keep my hands clean."

She giggles and I smile at the sound. "So you're like 50 percent troublemaker."

"Something like that. And what about you, Quinn Miller? Tell me why you haven't kept in touch with your parents."

"Well, I think it just boiled down to the fact that I required attention they didn't want to take away from their work. And after the horrific graduation party, they told me to get out, that they didn't sign up for this when they became parents. It also didn't help that I had no desire to study science and that I turned down all of my college acceptance letters. I knew what I wanted to do with my life, and I was determined to make it happen. I'm one of the lucky ones in this industry."

"They don't deserve you, you know?"

"Who?"

"Your parents. If they couldn't support you, then they don't deserve you."

"Thanks for saying that, Trevor."

Our plates scraped clean, I reach over and snag the papers on the table.

"So, how does this work?"

"I'll read the part I'll be playing, and you can read the opposing characters."

"I see. Do we need to act out anything or just read what's written?"

"I tend to move around to feel the story, but you don't have to."

Nodding, I set our plates in the sink for washing later. She follows me from the kitchen to the living room, where I take a seat on the couch while Quinn continues to stand.

"There's a second copy under the binder clip. Could you hand it to me?"

The papers remain steady in my hands even though internally my nerves are shaking.

"Thanks," Quinn cheerfully replies. "So, you'll start off as Brian, the love interest and the boss, and I'm playing Kaitlyn, the disgruntled employee. We can start at scene two, since the opening is just a monologue. This is a romantic comedy, so timing, for me, will be everything."

"Got it."

"I'm not sure how much longer I can take this anymore, Jennifer. How does he think he can get away with this? Firing 80 percent of the staff in his first week? His ego must be the largest thing about Brian Jenkins."

Completely enraptured by the way she transformed into the role, I almost miss my line.

"Did I hear my name?"
"No, sir."
"I'm sure I did. Please step into my office Ms...."
"Ms. Hartwell. Kaitlyn Hartwell."

The scene continues to unfold before my eyes, but I'm completely fascinated with Quinn and her abilities. She isn't just good, she's amazing at her craft.

"Whew, do you think I can get a water?" she says after a while. "My throat is getting dry."

"Sure, I'll grab us some glasses. Anything else you'd like?"

"Chocolate?" she jokes as she goes back to reading over the next scene in the script.

In the kitchen, I fill our glasses from the tap just as a bright light flashes outside the window and a rumble vibrates the house.

"Shit," I murmur as I make my way back to the living room, remembering how much a certain someone hates storms. When I find her clutching the script as if her life depends on it, I guess her fear hasn't diminished.

"Quinn, are you still freaked out by thunder and lightning?" I ask as I place the glasses on the coffee table.

"No, of course not," she responds just as the lights flicker, then extinguish completely. "I lied, I'm still scared of storms."

Carefully walking over to where she'd been standing, I reach out in the hopes of finding her. She yelps just as my fingers touch her arm, then mutters an apology.

"Come here, sweetheart."

She follows my command and presses her shaking body against my chest. Another flash of lightning brightens the room, and I look down into her terrified eyes. I don't recollect the reason behind her fear, but I'm sure it has to do with neglectful parents and a young girl having to weather the storm herself. Her eyes instantly change from fear to desire as they focus on my lips.

Fuck, I want to kiss her so bad I can feel it in my bones. I thrust my hands into her hair and tilt her head back.

"Quinn, I'm going to make something perfectly clear. When I kiss you, you will be mine for however long you're here. Nothing more, just sex. Can you handle that?"

God, I hope she can.

"I have no plans to stay in Dale City. Just sex. I can handle it."

Frantically, I lean forward and seal my lips with hers, her beautiful plump lips brushing against mine. There is no slow start, just a desperate plea to taste as much of her as possible.

Lightning flashes again, and I pull away from her slightly and reach down to scoop her into my arms with the intentions of carrying her to my bedroom.

The house rumbles just as I set her on top of the duvet. Slowly, I remove each sandal from her delicate feet and make my way up the bed to rest my body on top of hers. Her hand snakes into my hair and tugs my head toward her mouth, where she seductively sucks on my bottom lip as her hips rock against my leg.

"Damn, baby."

Her neck calls to me, and I move my lips farther down to suck on the sweet skin at her pulse point, earning me a cry of want. While she's distracted, I glide my hand up her arm, then slowly trail the strap of her dress over her shoulder and down to her elbow until one of her pert breasts is exposed before repeating the move on the other side.

"Trevor," Quinn whimpers.

"Don't worry, sweetheart. I'm going to make you feel good."

I move my mouth from her neck and trace a path down to her left nipple as I reach up to caress her right breast. The weight is incredible in my hold, and I have to control the urge to squeeze it too harshly. A gasp escapes her mouth and she arches her back as I suck and nip on the blush-colored pebble.

Equal opportunistic man that I am, I turn my attention to the other breast and repeat the same motions.

Quinn continues to squirm under me and I push her dress up, allowing my leg to rest more firmly at her core. Through my shorts, I can feel how wet she is, and it turns me on even more. My cock strains for attention beneath my zipper.

"Do you want more, sweetheart?"

Her hands skirt underneath my shirt, easing it up my chest. I help her remove it and watch in the darkness as her chest rises and falls at a faster pace. Her hands explore my body, taking her time to dip in and out of each divot between the muscles. My nipples painfully harden as she tugs on the piercings with her delicate fingers.

"Fuck, that feels good, baby," I growl and rub my erection against her soaked center.

She begins to reach for my zipper, but I know if she so much as touches my cock, I'll lose it and fuck her senseless. Normally I would have no qualms about this, but Quinn is my friend—well, at one time and place we were best friends. And she doesn't need to be treated like the women I'm normally with. She needs to be treated with the care she deserves.

Placing my hand on top of hers, I reluctantly halt her movements.

"Quinn, I want to make you feel good."

A magnetic draw seals our lips together once more, and our tongues taste the incredible flavor of each other's mouths. The smooth skin of her legs explodes in goose bumps as I slide my hand up her thigh. I'm surprised when I come in contact with what appears to be a simple pair of panties. She's flaunted her body in thongs and less in magazines, so to find that she isn't that girl she's made out to be makes me smile against her lips.

The waistband sits low on her hips and I trace the elastic material back and forth, letting the tips of my fingers dip past the barrier. Her teeth nibble at my lip, and I take that as a suggestion to continue further. Beneath the panties, I'm welcomed with a heated wet center.

"So fucking wet for me, sweetheart."

The folds welcome my fingers and I glide them back and forth, making sure to pay extra attention to the swollen bundle of nerves peeking out from beneath its hood. The muscles in her legs begin to quiver, and I know she's getting closer to her precipice.

"Are you going to come, baby?"

As she nods in reply, I slide one and then two fingers deep into her slit, stroking relentlessly.

"Fuck," she shouts, her head rearing back and her body arching.

Her core clamps down onto my digits and my erection grows to painful measures. I continue to stroke and rub her sex to help Quinn ride out her orgasm.

Then my phone rings on the nightstand, the flashing name on the screen like a downfall of cold water on our moment.

Quinn jumps from the bed and quickly adjusts her clothes.

"Oh my God, how could we forget about Izzy? She's going to flip out. Trevor," she says frantically, "she can *not* know about this. It would kill her."

Hands up in surrender, I calmly assure, "Hey, don't worry, I won't say a word. We'll just have to sneak around, that's all. Can you handle that?"

"I don't know. She's my best friend, Trevor."

"I was once your best friend too."

"I know," she says as she makes her way to the front door, swinging it widely only to come face-to-face with a downpour.

"Quinn, I can take you home."

"I'll be fine. It's just across the street."

"Quinn," I sigh as she steps out onto the porch and farther into the rain. "Quinn, you're mine!" I shout above the sound of the downpour.

"You're fucking mine," I whisper to myself as I close the door behind her, praying Izzy doesn't find out because Quinn is right—it'll devastate her.

CHAPTER SEVEN
Quinn

*H*AIR PLASTERED TO MY face, I head into Izzy's house looking like a drowned rat.

Hurriedly I rush into my bedroom, doing my best to ignore the storm whirling outside, and the one whirling inside of me.

I've never let go like that before. The way Trevor was able to possess my body with just the lightest touch of his fingers was something I had only read about, but having it happen to me personally left me reeling.

As I pull the soaked dress from my body, a shiver trembles down my spine, not from the cold but from my skin sensitivity. Needing to clear my mind, I plop onto my bed and lie back, letting the darkness surround me.

My body still craves Trevor's touch; it's strung so tightly I feel like it'll break at any moment.

I listen closely for any noises but hear nothing but the sound of rain pounding away on the roof. Within the blackness, I make out my duffel bag and an idea forms in my mind. I search through the bag and practically whimper when I can't locate what I'm looking for, but then I find it underneath a pair of shorts.

Triumphantly I carry the vibrator back to the bed, where I relax against the cool sheets. Closing my eyes, I allow visions of Trevor and the way he commanded my body to take over. One of my free hands works its way to my breasts, gently squeezing the masses as I slide the vibrator through my still-slick folds. I envision the way our mouths had sealed together as if possessed by a needy desire. The way his fingers delicately traced each inch of my skin. The way he seemed to want me just as much as I wanted him.

I slide the vibrator in and out of my heated center, rubbing it across my clit at every pass.

I moan as another release builds in my core. Picturing Trevor's impressive cock slipping in and out of my sex, I detonate with his name on my lips.

Completely spent, and now with the realization that we have no water without the power on, I set the vibrator aside with the hope that I remember to wash it tomorrow. Another crash of lightning soars across the sky, followed by a pounding of thunder.

The front door opens and closes quickly, and then I hear a knock at my bedroom door.

"Are you okay, Quinn?" Izzy asks as she peeks around the door, and I'm thankful I had the chance to throw the covers over my body.

"I'm fine, thank you. I'm just hanging out in here."

"I didn't expect you home yet. How did the read-through go?"

"Really well. Trevor was very helpful." Amongst other things.

"Good, I'm glad to hear it. I'll make sure Mom knows. Anyway, did you eat? I was going to call in a delivery."

"I did, actually. Trevor cooked me dinner."

"He did?"

My eyes widen in surprise at the callousness of her tone.

"Well, he made it for himself, but he had some left when I got there and I hadn't eaten yet," I try to explain with a smidgen of a lie that burns as it escapes my lips.

"Hmm... okay. I just know how my brother is and I mean, you're my best friend. I'm not entirely sure it's so smart for you both to spend time alone together."

"Why would you say that?" I sit up straighter on the bed as Izzy rests against the doorjamb.

"I mean, if he acts like the usual asshole he is, you may leave earlier, and I want you here as long as possible."

"Well, he was nothing but nice to me, so no worries there. You have nothing to worry about, Izzy. You know I'm married to my career. I don't have time to deal with a playboy."

"That's true. Hey, do you want to head into town with me tomorrow for all-you-can-eat tacos at the Taco Stand?"

"Tacos? Girl, you know I'm there."

"All right, well I know the storm is going to keep you up, so if you want to borrow my Kindle, you're welcome to. I have a few paperbacks I plan on diving into."

"I brought a few books with me, so I'm good, but thank you. Oh, where can I find some candles?"

"Oh, right. There are some in the hall closet. I'll grab them for you."

A few minutes later, the bedroom is illuminated with the help of a few matches and some strategically placed candles. Izzy takes a minute to glance around the space, her eyes narrowing and then widening in surprise when her gaze lands on the bright pink vibrator I tossed on my duffel bag.

"Do I want to know?"

I laugh and then joke, "It keeps me calm during the storm."

"Well, don't let me get in your way. Just… be quiet."

I continue laughing as Izzy exits the room and loudly closes the door.

That night I toss and turn as the storm continues to roll outside the window. It must've triggered something inside of me, because I spend the night dreaming about the last time Izzy, Trevor, and I had made it out to the clearing in the middle of the fields.

We kick up dirt as we step along the worn tracks left by a tractor. Behind us, Trevor carries a small bag with our confiscated items inside, while Izzy and I both carry a blanket.

Finally making our way to the clearing, Izzy and I set up the blankets while Trevor uncaps the bottle of Boone's Farm. I'm mesmerized as the sinewy muscles in his forearms twist with the corkscrew, each vein popping with the movement.

"Hello, Quinn," Izzy remarks, trying to get my attention. When she notices my eyes trained on Trevor, she snaps her fingers. "Don't even think about it. You know how he is."

"I wasn't thinking about anything," I reply innocently as I walk over to a level spot and lie down on my blanket beside Izzy's.

"Sure you weren't. He would destroy you, Quinny. You're inexperienced, and he knows more than most adults."

"Izzy, that's your brother, and you're just as inexperienced."

"I know, but he's still a man whore. Plus, how awkward would it be? Remember when Kelly started dating her brother's best friend?"

"Yeah, they broke up six months later and her parents had to send Liam to military school after he practically strangled Mike."

"See? How awful would it be if I had to choose sides? He's my twin, we share something special, but you're my bestie."

"I know," I hesitantly concede. "Plus, it's not like he would want anything to do with me anyway."

Trevor bends over to grab the plastic cups from the bag and fill them with the cheap berry wine, then stalks over to us, two cups and his flask dangling between his fingers.

"I'd like to make a toast," he states as he takes a seat next to me on the blanket. "To the start of our sophomore year and to a lifetime of friendship."

We finish the two bottles of Boone's Farm while Trevor takes sips from his flask filled with an amber liquid. The stars seem brighter this night as we lie on our backs, gazing up into the sky. Suddenly a shooting star passes across the blackened horizon and I make the wish of all wishes, that one day Trevor and I could be together without destroying Izzy. It's a silly *wish, full of hope and dreams and a schoolgirl crush, but it was* my *hope and dreams, and my heart knew what it wanted.*

My spirit soars when at the same time, he reaches over and laces his fingers through mine. A gesture not unfamiliar, but this time it feels very different. Perhaps my wish will come true after all.

Unfortunately, two weeks later when school begins, I'm faced with the reality that my wish is like those of many before—a waste. Though Izzy and I are as close as ever, Trevor pays us no mind while in school, even when he and I share classes together. It hurts the way he ignores me in the hall, and even more so when he doesn't join Izzy and me in the clearing any longer.

When I ask her what changed, she shrugs, "I told you not to crush on him. He was bound to hurt you, Quinn. Especially with the rotation of cheerleaders he's been keeping occupied recently. Just be glad you didn't fall in love. Imagine how that would have ended."

With a start, I wake up and gasp for air. I had forgotten the details of that night, just remembering that Izzy had laid down the line on Trevor and me ever pursuing anything together. He had made it clear that he wanted nothing from me, except now I'm confused with the hand holding. It had felt different that night. His thumb had brushed my knuckles as we all stared into the twinkling sky, but my experience was too limited to know what to do with the fact that he was touching me in more than a friendly manner.

"Shit," I murmur into the dark room. It's only an hour past midnight and I need to get some sleep, but I'm not sure I can rest after that. From the nightstand, I grab one of the candles and strike a match, holding it to the wick to illuminate the room.

I move into the living room and peer out the window. Luckily the storm has stopped. Just as I'm about to step away, I notice a flame flicker in the upper window of Trevor's house. Strange that he would be awake at the same time I am. I wonder if he was plagued by the same dream, or if something else keeps him awake at night.

Resting my head on the cool glass, I imagine what would've happened had Izzy not called Trevor while we were on the bed. I've never had one-night stands or slept with a man I didn't have a relationship with, but with the way I was losing the fight against my body, I would've allowed Trevor to devour me completely. Body and soul.

I always knew he was more than he let people see, especially after learning that he took the blame for actions he didn't commit. And in the past two days since I've been back, the town seems to sing his praises. A far cry from how they acted toward him as a teenager. They had treated him like the town pariah at sixteen, but to me, he had always been that shy thirteen-year-old boy who stood behind his overzealous sister as she welcomed me to Dale City.

With my eyes trained on the window overlooking the front yard, I move toward the couch and curl up under one of the blankets. I had promised him that my feelings wouldn't get involved, and I pray I'm able to keep that promise, but I fear I'm going to fail.

I'm not sure they ever went away to begin with.

RENEE HARLESS

CHAPTER EIGHT
Trevor

*T*HE OFFICE IS EERILY quiet for a Tuesday evening. Paperwork stacks high on my desk with no end in sight as I begrudgingly reach for another file. Having to carry the weight of two other officers we have yet to hire is starting to drain me. But tomorrow I finally get a day off, and I told the chief that I have no intentions of turning my phone on. And if all goes to plan, I'll be spending the day in bed with Quinn.

She had surprised the hell out of me when I realized how sensitive she was to my touch. My fingers yearned to feel every millimeter of her skin, and her kiss... God, her kiss was as potent as any drug.

The chair squeaks as I lean back, paperwork long forgotten as I tug at my pants to give space to my growing erection. I guess it's a good thing the office is empty, or my coworkers would be getting an eyeful.

Taking a few breaths, I calm myself down and focus back on the stack of papers on my desk when I hear the door chime.

"Hey, man," a male voice greets.

"Hey, Vic. Come on back."

Vic's been here enough that he knows how to get to my office. He actually works part-time with the police department and spends the rest of his time taking care of his ailing grandmother. He looks menacing, with his heavily tattooed body and dark gaze, but he has a heart of gold.

As Vic enters the office, his eyes triple in size at the stack of work in front of me.

"Busy day?"

"Busy month. With the shortage, I seem to be in charge of picking up the slack."

"Well shit, that sucks. You need some help?"

"I'm off tomorrow, finally. It's been like two months without a single day of rest and relaxation. If you want to come in on Thursday, I really would appreciate getting through this stack."

"No problem, but only under one condition."

"What's that?"

"You come with me to the Taco Stand tonight."

"Why?" I ask skeptically.

"Because they have tacos and half-price beers."

That does sound good, and my stomach must agree because it grumbles loudly, causing Vic to laugh.

"I guess I'm in."

We duck around the crowd as we walk into the restaurant. Luckily they part ways when I pass, either from fear of knowing I'm a cop or because I'm generally that intimidating. A few women who had warmed my bed previously send winks in my direction, but I ignore them. Those women can't hold a candle to Quinn.

And as if I conjured her up, I see my fantasy woman sitting at a table with my sister. I had thought about her all day, and my thoughts didn't do her any justice. Her blonde hair is tied high on her head with loose curls trailing down her back. Today she's wearing a simple T-shirt with a college emblem emblazoned across her chest and a pair of black shorts. I actually find myself grinning as I take her in, her appearance reminding me so much of the girl I grew up with.

Vic follows closely behind me as I make my way to their table.

"Good evening, ladies. Mind if we join you?" I ask, but my attention never wavers from Quinn, whose eyes have grown double in size.

"Sure," she whispers just as Izzy says, "No."

"Come on, Iz. We'll behave. And look, I even brought a friend."

The girls were sitting across from each other, leaving an open chair on either side. My focus rests completely on Quinn until a waitress comes by to take Vic's and my drink order.

"So, what are you girls going to eat?"

"Uh, tacos," Izzy rudely announces, irritation seeping through her tone. But as I glance up, I'm surprised to find Vic enraptured by her. Which sort of freaks me out because although Isabel and I are fraternal twins, we look very similar. Luckily, Quinn takes that moment to ask me how my day at work was, and my ruminations regarding my sister are put to rest.

"Good. Busy."

"I'm sorry to hear that." She takes a hearty sip of her oversized margarita with a beer tipped over into the glass. "Do you get a break anytime soon?"

"Why, Quinn? Are you propositioning me?" I twist my body completely in her direction and lean into her space. Her cheeks flush with a beautiful pink color and her plump lips hang open in surprise.

"N-no. I was just won—"

"It's all right, Quinn. I'm just messing with you. But yes, I do have a day off tomorrow, and I told the chief that he isn't allowed to contact me for anything unless it's an absolute emergency."

"Oh, I don't have plans for anything tomorrow. Would you want to practice the script with me?"

"Sure." I lean closer to her body, her breath hitching the closer I get. "And I plan on doing a lot more than just read through a bunch of words with you."

Her face reddens even further, and I chuckle as I lean back in the chair, completely content with how she reacts to me.

"Hey, Trevor," Izzy pipes up.

I turn to face her and raise my eyebrow for her to continue as I take a sip of my beer.

"Are you still off from work tomorrow?"

"Yeah, why?" I skeptically ask, praying she isn't about to squash my day of having Quinn in my bed.

"Don't forget you're joining me at the Dale City Assisted Living Facility tomorrow to volunteer."

"Ah, fuck."

I'd completely forgotten, which is a shock because volunteering there is one of my favorite things to do. Some of the seniors are the funniest people I've ever met. I thread my hand through my hair, gripping the ends before sliding it down my face in exasperation.

"Shit, I'm sorry, Iz. I forgot. But I'll be there." Begrudgingly I turn my attention back to Quinn, who has her straw between her lips, pretending she isn't paying attention to the conversation. But knowing her the way I do, I can tell she's disappointed.

My shaking hand reaches out and grasps her elbow, pulling her attention toward me.

"Hey," I coax softly. "I'm sorry, Quinn. Maybe we can get together after?"

"Sure, yeah. It's totally fine. I'll probably just spend the day sleeping in. I haven't done that in a while."

Absentmindedly, I run my fingers up her arm and then trail them back down.

"Hey, why don't you join us?" Vic proposes.

"Us?" Izzy scoffs, but I can see the gleam of interest in her eyes.

Her and Vic? That would be an interesting pair. All-American cheerleader and the leather-clad bad boy. At least I know he would take good care of her.

"Well, I mean I'll be there with my grandmother anyway. They can always use more volunteers," Vic explains to a stunned Izzy while I train my attention back to Quinn.

"That's a great idea, Vic. What do you say, Quinn? Want to spend the day helping us?" I grin.

"Sure, that sounds like fun. I enjoy volunteering."

"And hey, I bet they'd love a live performance from the amazing Quinn Miller. We could do the read-through there for a bit."

Before Quinn can shoot down the option, Izzy perks up and announces what a great idea it is just as the stack of fifty tacos makes its way to the table.

"Were you planning on feeding an army?" Vic asks as he grabs a taco from the top and I reach for one in the middle, almost as if we're playing an adult version of Jenga.

"We were hungry, and whatever we had left over we were going to bring to your office, brother dearest."

"Really? That surprises me, Iz, since rarely do you think of bringing me dinner."

"Oh, don't worry, I haven't changed my stripes. It was all Quinn's idea."

The taco crunches in my mouth as I take a hearty bite and focus on Quinn, who daintily holds her taco over her plate, taking small nibbles.

"You were going to bring me food?"

Her narrow shoulders move up and down in a shrug, and damn if I don't feel warm inside knowing she was thinking of me. I stare at her until her eyes peek from their corners and focus on me, then smile broadly and flash her the lone dimple on my right cheek.

"Thank you, sweetheart."

Forty-five minutes later, we all slouch back in our chairs, table littered with beer bottles and a few extra-large margarita glasses, as well as two lone tacos sitting on the silver platter.

Enjoying the bickering between Izzy and Vic as they fight over someone needing to finish the last two tacos and not letting them go to waste, I turn my head to watch Quinn as she sits back with an oversized smile on her face. On its own accord, my hand slips from my lap and moves onto Quinn's bare thigh. I squeeze the muscle gently until her gaze slides over to meet mine.

As much as I want to slide my fingers up between the apex of her thighs, I can't risk Quinn's privacy. Instead, I smirk at her until she places her hand over mine to stop my fingers from creeping higher. Itching to touch her, I flip my hand over and intertwine our fingers together. Many previous girlfriends had tried to hold my hand, but none had ever felt right. Nothing like how it feels to hold Quinn's.

Her soft delicate palm pressed against the rough skin of my own takes me back to the last time I held her hand, the last time we were together, the last time we were just friends. Because I knew that night in the clearing as we peered up at the stars that she would never again be just a friend. She had a place in my heart that I would keep locked away tight, a precious piece of me that I never wanted to be destroyed.

Our eyes lock once more, and she smiles that beautiful, innocent smile I've come to love. Not the one she shares with her millions of fans, the one she keeps secret. The one that speaks of joy and love.

At that moment, the loud bustle of the restaurant dies away and it's just me and Quinn, two kids who couldn't have been more different but were the best of friends at one time. I want to lean down and kiss her, but with Izzy sitting across from us, I hesitate.

Quinn lowers her eyes to our hands and squeezes our fingers gently. Then, surprising me and probably the rest of the restaurant, she scoots closer to me and leans over to rest her head on my shoulder. Her eyes are closed, making everyone believe she's just tired, and she very well may be, but she's also an incredible actress, and by the way she strokes the side of my hand with her thumb, I know she simply couldn't control her desire to be closer.

I watch in fascination as Izzy stops mid-sentence and turns her attention to us. Vic simply chuckles and takes a sip of water while Izzy's eyes narrow in anger but then they soften as she believes Quinn's lie.

"Trevor," Izzy admonishes until I shake my head.

"She said she was tired. I guess I could take her home."

"We were going to take an Uber since we were drinking. You have been too."

"I'll call a car for all of us."

"That's okay," Vic says. "I haven't had but the two beers and water, but I'll see you all tomorrow."

"All right, see ya, Vic."

I check to see what kind of vehicle will be arriving for us and relay the information.

"Izzy, I'll take care of the check and Quinn if you can go wait for the car? I'm sure Vic wouldn't mind waiting with you."

Their attention never wavers, but Izzy says, "Sure, I can do that," as Vic helps her from her seat.

The breath against my neck remains slow and steady, and for a moment I think Quinn really has fallen asleep. But as if she has a sixth sense that Izzy and Vic have left, her eyes fly open and she straightens in her seat.

"Are they gone?"

Without waiting for a response, she brings both of her slender hands to my face and seals our lips together.

It's a small kiss, merely a peck, but she pours herself into it, and I can't help but take everything offered.

"Fuck, I thought you really had fallen asleep."

"And that, my friend, is why I am an award-winning actress."

And in a moment of unbridled fear, I begin to wonder if she's acting with me. But she couldn't be, not my Quinn.

As if she can hear my thoughts, she presses another soft kiss to my lips. "Never with you, Trevor. Never with you."

The sincerity floating in her eyes warms me, reminds me of what we can never have. *No feelings. This is just sex. Getting rid of the desire for someone you've wanted since you were a teenager.*

Tossing a few twenties on the table, I escort her outside where the Uber is waiting. Of course, I don't mention to Izzy that we catch her lip-locked with my friend. That's a blackmail for another day.

Back at the girls' house, we exit the car. I hadn't been able to steal any more moments with Quinn since Izzy told me to ride shotgun.

"We'll, um, see you tomorrow," Quinn explains as she follows Izzy into the house. For a moment I consider running in after them, since I do have a copy of the key, but I know it would be a risk for Quinn. Izzy would definitely find out. Instead, I find myself sulking back to my house, where I plop down on the couch in the blackness. Simply staring out the window, I lull myself into a haze of nothingness but the ticking clock on the wall.

"Fuck," I shout as I realize I'm craving her.

Hopping from the couch, I dash out the front door and back to my sister's house. Figuring that Quinn is in the back-facing guest room, I head in that direction. A lamp shines in the window, and then I see Quinn's shadow against the wall. The window sits up a little bit higher on this end of the house, so I glance around the backyard for something to stand on.

Jackpot. Grabbing the small gardening stool by the back door and praying it holds my weight, I move it under the window and steady myself before tugging at the window, surprised that it moves. As the window reaches its stopping point, I place my hands on the sill just as Quinn walks back into the room.

"Don't scream," I whisper just as Quinn lets out a yelp before covering her mouth.

She glances out into the hall and then promptly closes the door before she makes her way over to me.

"What are you doing here?"

I struggle to get my large body through the window, and as I make it about halfway, I realize my mistake. I'm now stuck and in an awkward position.

I look up at Quinn and find her giggling behind her hand before I sullenly ask her for a little help. She tugs me forward until I clumsily drop onto the floor, both silent for a moment as we hear Izzy's footsteps approaching.

"Are you all right in there, Quinn?"

"Yes, sorry. I tripped over my bag but I'm fine."

"Oh, okay. Good night."

"Night," Quinn replies before she rushes over to help me off the floor. "What are you doing here, Trevor?"

"I… I don't know. I just wanted to see you."

"Well, you could've just video messaged me, silly."

She's right, but I needed to see her in person.

"I needed to come over, Quinn," I declare as I step closer to her, sliding my hands under her oversized shirt and placing them on her hips.

"Why?" she chokes out on a whisper as our bodies come flush against one another.

"So I could do this."

I skim a hand up her back as I lean forward, capturing her lips. Her taste is sweet and minty, reminding me of a cool breeze along the boardwalk at the beach.

"Trevor," she whispers against my mouth as she reaches out for my shirt, tugging it from my pants. "I need you."

Our bodies pull apart, each of us dropping our hands to hang loosely.

"Can you keep quiet, Quinn?" I ask, and she nods enthusiastically. "Good," I reach behind me to gather the material of my shirt in my fists and yank it over my head, tossing it to the side.

Her eyebrows rise on her forehead, giving her a doe-eyed expression as she stares at my naked chest. It's as if she's seeing it for the first time, and for some reason that makes me feel good. Because I know that once I have her naked and underneath me, it'll be as if it's the first time for me too.

"Tit for tat, sweetheart." I wave toward her shirt.

Her pearly straight teeth bite down on her peach-colored lip as her gaze drops to the floor.

"I want you to do it," she says barely above a whisper. If I hadn't been listening closely, I would've missed it.

"Anything for you, sweetheart."

Stepping closer to her again, I clutch the soft material of her shirt in my fingers, watching in rapture as she raises her arms and I remove the material. Each peak of her breasts hardens under my gaze as I place my hands on her back and stroke her soft skin up and down.

"Mmm, that feels good," she assures as her eyes close and her head falls back in bliss.

Licking a trail from the base of her neck up to her ear. I smile against her skin as her body shivers.

"I bet I know how to make you feel even better."

"Mmm," she moans, reaching out to grasp my waist.

Moving so my mouth hovers over her lips, I whisper her name until her eyes shoot open.

"There you are. I want you looking at me when I make you come apart, sweetheart."

After pressing a kiss to her lips, I drop to the floor and rest my knees on the soft material of the rug and run my hands up and down Quinn's toned legs, swirling my hand toward her center whenever I approach that point. I can easily feel the heat exuding from her body with every pass, and it has my mouth watering. Unable to control my desire, I reach up and yank her panties down her legs, bringing me face-to-face with one of my favorite parts of her body.

Leaning forward, I run my nose across the front of her mound, taking in the sweet smell of her juice. A groan escapes my chest as she grips my hair. When I slide my finger through her folds, that grip tightens almost painfully, but I welcome it. The pain will keep me grounded, because I seriously run the risk of losing myself to Quinn indefinitely.

After spreading her legs farther apart, my fingers and tongue explore her center. Her legs begin to shake and I find myself smiling against her clit as I suck it into my mouth.

"Trevor." Her voice quivers as she presses my head further toward her center, where I lave at her folds in time with the thrusting of my fingers.

My cock grows excruciatingly hard in my pants, but I ignore the agony. My goal is to make Quinn fall apart, and I won't quit until she does. My pleasure is secondary to hers.

It doesn't take long for her body to convulse around my fingers as her knees practically give out beneath her. I scoop her into my chest and carry her to the bed. She leans forward and tugs on my earlobe with her teeth, sending a spark of electricity straight to my cock.

"Are you ready for me?" I ask as I remove my shoes and socks, then tug down my pants and underwear in one swoop.

"Yes. I need you, Trevor."

I waste no time aligning my cock with her entrance, sliding the stiff erection through her soaked folds. It feels heavenly and warm, and it's then that I remember that I'm missing something.

"Shit, condom," I complain as I move away from her body, but a gentle hand on my arm freezes my movements.

"I'm clean and on the pill, Trevor."

Tilting forward, I rest my head on her chest as relief floods through me.

"I'm clean too," I explain.

"I want this with you, Trevor. Only with you."

And fuck if I don't want the same.

Turning my head to the side, I press a kiss to one breast and then the other before I rear back onto my knees, spreading her bent legs wide. I stare at her pretty pink pussy as I glide my cock up and down the folds, coating it in its wetness, and all I can think is *Mine*.

Quinn's eyes grow heavy as I continue to tease her body, stroking my cock against her center and only putting an inch into her core before sliding right back out.

I can tell it's driving her crazy, but I want her crazed. I want the uninhibited version of Quinn that she keeps hidden away.

"Please, Trevor," she begs, her fingers clawing at the duvet as she rocks her hips against me, trying to slide my cock farther into her channel.

Her begging is my undoing and I thrust myself deep into her sheath, the tightness almost mind-blowing with the way it hugs my cock so strongly.

"Shit, baby, you're so tight," I growl as I pull back and slide back in again. "I'm not going to last long. You feel too good."

Quinn doesn't respond, just grips my thighs as she meets each of my thrusts until we're pounding against each other, our skin slickened with sweat. She greedily reaches down and places her fingers on her mound, rubbing her clit.

"You're fucking gorgeous like this." I grip her legs, pushing them toward her shoulders, then lean forward and suck a nipple into my mouth, earning a lustful gasp from Quinn as she begins to tighten.

Her eyes squeeze tightly shut and I smack a hand against her ass as I demand, "Open your eyes. I want to watch you when you come." She follows my command just as the waves of her pussy milk my cock.

"Fuck," I cry out as my release explodes into her core, thrusting a few more times, wanting to savor the feel of her body convulsing against mine.

Collapsing on top of her, I press a kiss against her smiling lips before I ask, "Are you okay?"

A dreamy sigh escapes her as I sink my hand into her wild hair, my cock still lodged deep within her body.

"That was amazing. I never knew."

"Never knew what, sweetheart?"

"That sex could be so wild and carefree."

My heart stops for a second while I consider her words.

"You're right," I remark as I remove myself from her hold, watching her confused eyes as she takes in my retreat. Without a word, I step out into the hall after making sure the coast is clear. In the bathroom, I wet a cloth with warm water and bring it back into the bedroom. My chest hurts when I see Quinn sitting up in her naked state but with her brows furrowed.

"Lie back," I say. "Let me clean you up."

She complies, and once I've finished removing my marking from her body, I pull back the covers and tuck her underneath.

Just as I'm tugging my shirt over my head, I hear the pained whisper coming from the bed.

"Did I do something wrong?"

And the ache in my chest almost cripples me as it intensifies. The look on her face could crush the mighty Zeus himself.

Shit.

Running my hands through my hair, I walk over to the bed and kneel beside her, running my knuckles across the smooth skin of her cheek. She practically purrs under my touch.

"I'm sorry, sweetheart. You didn't do anything wrong, but I'm afraid if I stay I'll never leave, and we don't want Izzy to find us in bed together."

"Izzy!" she whispers with shock-filled eyes. "I almost forgot all about her. You don't think she heard anything, do you?"

"Naw, she'd be down here kicking my ass if she did. Chicks before dicks and all that mess."

"Yeah, you're probably right. Sorry, I had a moment. It must've been the orgasm making my head all loopy."

Laughing under my breath, I assure, "It's fine. I should probably head back to my house anyway." Pressing my lips against hers once more, I let my mouth linger for an extra second, memorizing the feel of her lips and the flavor of her taste. "I'll see you bright and early tomorrow."

"Okay," she says as she yawns into the back of her hand, shimmying farther under the covers. Just as I hop up onto the window sill, I hear her say my name.

"Trevor, I wish you could stay tonight."

"Me too, sweetheart. Me too."

I plunge into the blackness of the night, wondering what kind of mess I just got myself into.

CHAPTER NINE
Quinn

LAST NIGHT WAS LIKE a dream come true, every one of my childhood fantasies come to life. Watching Trevor climb and then flounder through my window, I was a little bit lost and a lot full of lust and desire. He had taken me to heights of passion I had never known, never experienced, and now all I can do is stand under the warmth of the shower and revel in the feel of the droplets on my sensitive skin.

Izzy came to my room early this morning, fully intent on waking me up, but I beat her to it. Truthfully, I hadn't slept. I couldn't. My mind kept whizzing around with thoughts of Trevor's engorged member between my legs, his hands on my skin, his lips on my neck.

Even after one night, I was perilously close to losing it. Trevor is perfection—he knows it and I know it. Hell, the world knows it. He's a good guy wrapped in a bad boy exterior, and I want as much of him as I can get. Which brings me to trouble. The butterflies in my belly grow every time I think about him. And if he simply looks my way, you'd think I poured a sweet nectar into my stomach with the way those flutters bounce around.

But I can do this. I'm an actress, for God's sake. I know how to keep feelings from sprouting roots. And Trevor's just a man. A good-looking one at that, but he has two brains, one of which controls the majority of his actions. And I need to remember that, remember the way I had to watch him with his revolving door of girls throughout high school, remember the way he didn't even say goodbye when I left.

When the water begins to cool, I hastily turn off the faucet and grab the towel draped over the shower curtain rod. Snagging a second towel from the linen closet in the bathroom, I twist my hair into its folds and contain the mass on the top of my head. Securing the larger towel under my arms, I open the bathroom door and rush down the hall the air conditioning chilling my wet limbs—until I run directly into a large mass that's blocking my path to the guest room.

I look up, and up some more, and meet Trevor's green-eyed gaze. Different chills travel down my limbs as he visually inspects every inch of my body.

"Good morning, Quinn," his deep and husky voice taunts, his finger stroking along the edge of the towel where the material meets my upper breast. "You look surprised to see me."

"I am. I mean, I didn't expect you here so early, and with Izzy walking around."

He shrugs carelessly, as if the potential of Izzy discovering us together in the hall means little to him.

"If you'll excuse me," I say as I try to brush by him, but he stands just as stoically as ever. "I would like to get dressed, Trevor."

With one final push, I spin past him, but not before he snags the towel just as I enter the room. I gasp as my now-naked body is exposed to the coolness of the air, my nipples hardening even further, almost painfully.

"Trevor!" I whisper, not wanting to draw his sister's attention, and then I slam the door in his face with him still holding the towel.

"Such a shame," I hear him whisper, then listen as his footfalls take him down the hall and away from the room.

Not sure what to wear to the assisted living facility, I try to think back to what Trevor was wearing— but let's be honest, I saw right through his clothes and imagined how he looked while he was naked above me last night. Settling on a blue jersey dress, I slide it over my body and then quickly braid my hair to keep it off my face.

A few minutes later, I stroll into the kitchen to find Trevor casually flipping something in a pan that smells like French toast and Izzy relaxing in her chair, knees bent and resting against the edge of the table.

"Hey, Iz. Hey, Trevor." I try to keep the redness off my cheeks as I think about the way he stripped me of the towel just moments ago.

"I'm surprised you're up so early. Don't you want to sleep in during your vacation?" Trevor asks with a smirk on his lips.

"Well, I had a *hard* time falling asleep last night. And when I work, I'm usually up before the sun rises, just FYI," I remind him with a bit more attitude than was probably necessary.

His eyes narrow as they make contact with mine, and then he lets them trail up and down my body as if inspecting produce for the ripest in the bunch. This time his gaze doesn't make me feel that delicious heat between my legs; instead I feel slimy, almost degraded, as if I am nothing more than one of many.

I quickly take a seat at the table and snag a banana from the basket in the center, my fingers shaking as I peel it.

"I made you breakfast," Trevor grumbles angrily as he sets a plate in front of Izzy and then me.

I'm not sure what set him off, probably the way I didn't take his crap a moment ago, but I don't deserve to be spoken to as if I'm an insolent child.

Dropping the banana onto the table, I grab his wrist just as he turns away and bring his attention back to me.

"Thank you."

I don't expect it, but his features soften and he utters, "You're welcome," just as he goes back to making a plate for himself.

Gripping the butter knife from the dish in front of me, I slice the banana onto my toast and take a hearty bite. The softness of the bread mixed with the egg and cinnamon explodes in my mouth, and I let out an ungraceful moan that finally brings Izzy's attention to the food on the table.

"I'm guessing it's good?" she asks, breaking off a piece and stuffs it into her mouth as she swipes across the screen on her tablet.

"This is really good, Trevor. Just don't tell my agent I'm eating like this. She'll have me on a juice cleanse faster than Hollywood couples get divorced."

And that reminds me that I probably need to check in with Priscilla. It's rare for us to go this long without speaking. Hell, normally we don't go longer than two hours.

Priscilla has been my agent since I moved to Los Angeles. She found me working at a local coffee shop, like many acting dreamers, and booked me an acting gig the next week. I've been lucky, because she's also someone I consider a friend. She looks out for me and takes care of me as if I'm her child, which, for someone who grew up in a house where I never felt wanted, is a nice feeling.

The room falls into silence as we each enjoy the breakfast Trevor prepared. I glance around the average-sized kitchen with white cabinets and stainless-steel appliances, very neutral and very un-Izzy. I hadn't noticed the other day, but the longer I stay in the house, the longer I feel that the place is detached from my friend.

Finally, I'm drawn to the mass of body heat permeating in the space beside me. Green eyes bore into me curiously, as if looking for something that isn't there. Our eyes lock and a wave of sincerity filters through his irises, an apology on the tip of his lips.

Instead, I break the stare and turn my attention across the way. "Hey, Iz, how come you don't have to work today?"

"Well, I have to work the shift on Saturday morning, so I get to take today off, and I like volunteering at the center."

Taking another bite of my toast, I ask, "So, what can I expect while we're there? What kind of volunteering will we be doing?"

"Whatever they need help with, but usually we're just asked to socialize with the patients. Many of them don't get visitors very often, if at all, so they love when we visit. And they'll be in the presence of the remarkable Quinn Miller."

A blush rises on my chest and makes its way up to my cheeks at her flattery.

"But don't worry. The infatuation with you will die quickly when their very own protector, Trevor Shaw, graces them with his attendance. We may even get to see a few butt grabs."

"Oh, Trevor, do you have some admirers?" I jest as I prop an elbow on the table and rest my chin in my hands, smiling at him with a twinkle in my eye.

"I do, actually," he plays along, stretching his muscled arms above his body and then folding them behind his head, his biceps flexing with the movement, leaving me transfixed. "You'll have to watch out for Mr. and Mrs. Sampson. I'm pretty sure back in the day they used to be swingers. They always ask when I plan on bringing around a girl, and Mr. Sampson always gets this far-off look on his face."

"So? That doesn't make them swingers," I protest.

RENEE HARLESS

"Well, I also found them trying to pocket my handcuffs as they spoke with the Coleman couple, and they weren't very quiet about their intentions."

My eyes expand beyond their limits as I gasp in surprise. I had thought he was kidding, but now I'm not so sure. I look over at Izzy, who nods enthusiastically as she covers her mouth with her hand.

"I'm not sure if you're trying to pull one over on me or not, but can you please point them out when we get there so I can make sure I don't say anything or do something stupid?"

Trevor chuckles and then agrees, and I silently finish the breakfast hoping he was just pulling my leg; otherwise, I'm going to get up close and personal with some seniors who have a more active love life than I can ever dream of.

*

THE DALE CITY ASSISTED Living Facility was built after I moved away, so I wasn't sure what to expect. My comparison to a homeless shelter was completely off base though—this one in particular looks like a nice hotel, with plush carpets, freshly painted walls, and designer décor. It's nicer than the first apartment I stayed in before I made it big in the business, and I'm thoroughly impressed.

A shriek escapes my lips as I feel a tight pinch on my backside. Whirling around with the full intention of smacking someone, I startle when I come face-to-face with… air. I look down at an older woman hunched over her walker, staring at my ass.

"It's so firm," she mumbles. "Mine used to be firm like that." She picks up her walker and hobbles a few steps, then repeats her motion as she heads toward the small treats table.

"Hey, Quinn. Are you coming?" Trevor asks as he and Izzy stand at the check-in area.

"Sorry," I say as I make my way over to them, rubbing the now-sore spot on my ass.

"Are you okay?"

"Yeah, I think so. Even though I was just accosted by an old lady. But at least I can take the compliment. Apparently my behind is very firm."

With a tilt of his head, Trevor looks over my shoulder and down my back before assessing me slowly.

"Can't say she's wrong there. Maybe you'll let me verify later?"

Unable to keep the smile from growing on my lips, I turn to look down at the check-in sheet Izzy handed me as I walked over.

"Maybe," I whisper as I peer at him from behind my lashes, watching as his own smirk grows. Collectively I hear female-driven sighs from around the room and my grin widens. He definitely has more than one secret admirer.

"Hey, guys," a deep voice says from behind us as Vic approaches, his eyes never leaving Izzy. "I'm glad you guys could make it. Want to meet my gram first? She's dying to meet a real-life movie star. Even made me put on her lipstick."

"Really?" Izzy asks breathlessly, like she can't believe this large masculine man would do something so caring.

"Yeah, she likes to have her face on for guests. Come on." We follow as we drop off the paperwork on the desk and grab our visitor badges.

Vic knocks on the door before opening it widely, ushering us inside. I don't miss how his hand lingers on Izzy's back as he shuts the door behind him.

We're promptly introduced to Mrs. Calerone, who also seems to notice the way sparks are popping between Vic and Izzy. After about an hour of listening to Vic be embarrassed as she tells stories of him growing up, having raised him in Arizona until he graduated high school and she moved them closer to her sister in Houston, we all move back to the check-in area to find out where we're needed. And as expected, they request us to the social hall, where some of the residents are playing games or watching television.

Trevor sidles up next to me as Vic and Izzy move toward the area where residents are playing a board game.

"Hey, did you want to work on reading lines?" he asks as he tugs the rolled-up script from his back pocket.

How had I not noticed it there before?

"Sure. I think Vic's grandma and a few of her friends wanted to watch. I want to make it exciting for them, so would you mind running through scene three with me?" I ask, knowing full well it's the scene where Kaitlyn and Brian kiss for the first time. I figured if there was a time to test our chemistry, that time would be now.

"That's fine," he replies as he walks over to an open space in front of the windows and opens the script. I notice the moment he comes across the kiss, his eyes growing in size as he looks over to me and then to Izzy, who's luckily engrossed in a game with Vic and two other men.

Finding Mrs. Calerone in the hallway, I direct her and her friends into the social hall and help them set up chairs so they can watch the small performance.

"We're just doing a read-through, but I hope you enjoy it. The scene isn't long, but it's the first moment that Kaitlyn and Brian, the main characters, realize they have feelings for each other. The problem is that he's her boss and she hates him."

"Ooo, this sounds juicy. Like that soap opera they play on the television after lunch," Mrs. Calerone tells her friends gleefully.

In a soft whisper, Trevor asks if I need the script, but I shake my head. I've got the scene memorized; it's actually my favorite out of the entire script. The first kiss typically is, being a hopeless romantic and all.

I shake out my limbs as I walk around in a small circle, letting my body and mind become Kaitlyn, the beautiful hard worker who's had enough from her boss.

"Ms. Long, can I see you in my office?" Trevor's deep voice commands as he becomes the egotistical CEO Brian.

Kaitlyn doesn't acknowledge his request, just simply stands from her desk and follows behind him, noticing how his gray slacks pull tight against his behind. Something she's noticed more and more often.

Brian shuts the door behind them and gestures for her to take a seat as he rests against his desk of metal and glass.

"So tell me, Kaitlyn, why should I keep you on board? As you can see, in the past month it's been brought to my attention that your work has been suffering."

"Suffering? Mr. Sage—"

"Brian. Please call me Brian."

"Brian," she sneers, "I've been staying late every night since you cut staff, doing the projects of at least five other people who you let go and who haven't been replaced as of yet on top of tackling my own work. If my work is suffering, it isn't because of me, it's because of you." Kaitlyn stands and walks closer to Brian, her anger palpable in the air and filling the

room. "And furthermore, I wish you would stop taking your lack of skills as a CEO out on your employees. We're busting our asses here while you sit behind this desk cleaning house."

"Too bad your wishes aren't going to be granted, Kaitlyn."

"God, what is wrong with you? Don't you have any feelings? Don't you care that you've fired over 75 percent of this company from jobs they've held since they came out of college? These aren't just puppets, Brian, they're people too, with families to take care of."

"I'm sorry you feel that way."

"Well, I'm sorry I feel anything toward you," she proclaims before realizing the words have spilled from her mouth. Her hand goes up to block her lips and she takes a step back, nearly tripping over the chair in her earnest to leave, but Brian's hand lashes out, capturing her wrist.

"What do you feel toward me, Kaitlyn?" he asks as his thumb strokes her wrist.

"Hate. Disdain. Anger. Take your pick."

Tugging her closer, he brings them toe to toe, chest to chest, his steady breath mixing with her shaky one.

"I think you feel something else for me. Something you wish you didn't—attraction."

"I don't know what you're talking about."

"Yes you do. I can smell your arousal from here, I bet you aren't even wearing panties under that skirt of yours. Tell *me, Kaitlyn, if I kissed you right now, would you turn me in for harassment?"*

Her eyes widen in fear, and shock, and lust as he tilts his head toward hers and arches his hips closer to her pelvis, his erection evident.

"Would you, Kaitlyn?"

"No," she whispers as he seals his lips over hers.

No cautious lover, he slips his tongue between her parted lips and explores her mouth as if it's his dying wish. And perhaps it is, but she welcomes the intrusion. Welcomes her lack of resistance. Welcomes the theory that she's about to lose her job to the first man she's felt anything for in years — hate and lust.

A growing round of applause echoes in the room, bringing both me and Trevor back from our interlude. That was a close call, but now my body aches to finish what we started, and based on Trevor's dilated gaze, he wants the same.

"That was some kiss," Izzy concurs as she saunters our way with Vic hot on her heels.

"Young lady, that was more than just a kiss. That was real passion. I haven't seen chemistry like that since I lost my Bernie, God rest his soul. You two blew me away. You are one talented actress, Miss Quinn."

"Thank you, Mrs. Calerone."

Vic steers his grandmother and Izzy back toward her room, but under her breath, I hear Izzy mumble, "Just some kiss, my ass."

A soft grip steers my elbow, and I turn to find Trevor eyeing me warmly.

"Hey, they asked if we wouldn't mind folding some of the linens for them. Are you game?"

"Sure. Just lead the way."

Lead me anywhere you want.

RENEE HARLESS

CHAPTER TEN
Trevor

I STEER QUINN DOWN a few halls and corridors before we locate the space. A blast of heated air pours out of the laundry room and surrounds us as I open the door.

"Damn, it's like a sauna in there. Now I know why they asked us to help. Who in their right mind would take this on?" I whine as I take in the washers and dryers whirling with their packed loads.

Along the wall, we see bags of linens marked "clean" and drag one over to the counter running along one entire wall. We work in silence, each of us grabbing towels and sheets, folding the over-bleached white material.

"Crap, it's hot as hell in here," Quinn sighs as she wipes the sweat forming on her brow. She would look utterly miserable to anyone passing by, but fuck if she doesn't look just absolutely gorgeous with the slick skin and damp hair. I watch as a bead of sweat drips down the clavicle of her neck and travels between her breasts, seeping under the coverage of her dress.

I'm mesmerized. And fucking needing her more than my next breath.

I crumple the mass of sheets in my hands and toss it aside on the counter as I stalk toward Quinn. Her head whips around and she backs up against the wall as I corner her.

"Trevor?" Her voice trembles as I move closer.

"Fuck, you look beautiful like this. I want you now, Quinn. I need to have you."

"But someone could see," she tries to explain, but my mind is elsewhere, particularly on the heave of her breasts as they rise and fall with her breathing.

"Quinn, I don't care if the Pope walks by. I need you."

I snake my hand under her braid to the back of her neck and tilt her head back, drawing her attention solely to me. She gazes up at me, fire and heat penetrating me through her steady gaze. I slip my other hand under her skirt, stroking the slick skin of her legs.

A raptured moan vibrates in her chest, and I inwardly smile at her reaction. My sweet Quinn enjoys my hands on her body.

I bunch the material up to her waist and rock my hips against her, letting her feel what she does to me. The heat from her sex diffuses through my pants straight to my cock.

I rock into her a few times as I passionately meld our mouths together. Her taste is so sweet, like pure sugar.

Guiding my hand upward, I push her panties aside and slide my fingers through her slickness. It's addictive the way her body reacts. Quinn closes her eyes as I move inside her, bringing her closer to her precipice.

Suddenly her eyes open and she stares up at me as her hands push at my chest, causing me to step back. I wonder for a moment if I've done something wrong, but then Quinn's attention falls to my cock straining behind my pants and she drops to her knees before me, striking me mute.

Her eyes peer up at me, slightly unsure but heated at the same time as her hands work on their own accord to release the zipper and button on my pants. My cock whips out from the waistband of my boxer briefs as she tugs them down, and her attention falls onto the swollen head.

I groan as her small fingers wrap around my girth, barely able to contain it in her grip. Quinn's lips part slightly as she begins to move her hand up and down my shaft, twisting her palm slightly with each stroke. It's almost more than I can bear but indescribably wonderful at the same time, not just her tight fist but the fact that it's Quinn stroking me.

"Damn, Quinn." I toss my head back, the sweat that had been building upon my hairline now dropping down my back.

"Does this feel good? Am I doing it the way you like?"

"Baby, if you do it any better I'll be exploding all over you."

"Hmm," she murmurs. "I may like that."

And fuck, if I wasn't already on the verge of reaching an uncontrollable point with her, I sure as hell am now as she puts her mouth on me, tasting me, savoring me, craving me.

Her tongue swirls around the bulbous head before she releases it with a pop, her mouth greedily sucking my erection back into the warm abyss of her mouth. A light slurping noise sounds from the way her cheeks hollow out with every pass. I brace my hands on the cool wall when I feel the back of Quinn's throat against my cock. It's the most thrilling sensation I've ever had in my life, even more so than when I slid between her legs last night.

Which really has me wanting between her legs again.

"Stand up," I request breathlessly, my cock straining for her mouth as she stands on wobbly legs.

"What's wrong? Was it not good?" she asks, but I silence her with my mouth as I rotate us around and pin her against the wall.

"If it was any better I would go blind. I want you here, now."

"Okay." She nods but I have little patience for a reply as I stroke my hand between the juncture of her legs to find her soaked through her panties.

"You're ready for me, aren't you?"

"Always," she moans as I move the center of her panties aside and slide my hand against her wetness.

After I slick my hand in her heat, I stroke it along my cock, making it jump in my palm.

Gripping one of her thighs, I hold it over my arm as I bend slightly, guiding my cock into her tight sheath. Our moans chime in unison as I slide to the hilt and then pause, letting her sex expand as it takes all of me in and adjusts to my size.

I watch in awe as Quinn places her petite hands on my shoulders and rocks her body against mine, seeking more.

"Hold on, sweetheart." I grip the leg already nestled against my waist and then seize her other leg, bringing it around my waist.

She adjusts herself in this position, rising and then settling back down slowly. Far too slowly for my liking.

I thrust into her, wanting to go as far as possible. Wanting her to feel me between her legs tonight, tomorrow, next week. Wanting her to remember where I've been when she leaves.

"Fuck, Quinn. You feel so God damn good. Tighter somehow."

Her channel squeezes me momentarily and I freeze.

"Kegels," she whispers. "You keep moving and I'll keep doing it."

She doesn't have to ask me twice. I readjust my hold on her thighs, spreading them wide, and plunge into her hard and fast. Our breaths mix in staccato beats, harmonizing with the distinctive whirl of the washers and dryers. The sweat pours down our bodies as our fevered passion intensifies.

"Trevor," she cries out as her nails dig into my shoulders.

"Come for me, Quinn," I command as my balls pull tight, a tingling in my spine growing rapidly

She makes it through a few more thrusts before she constricts around me forcefully, pulling me so tightly that it causes me to erupt instantly. I jerk as the pulsations race through me, unable to control my body's reaction.

"Damn," I grunt as I slide out of her warmth and immediately have a sense of loss.

As I place her legs gently back onto the floor, her eyes are closed, her chest heaves with deep breaths, and her high cheeks are reddened from the heat and exertion. But the thing that captures my eye the most is the tiniest of smiles on her lips. Just a tip of the corners upward, enough to let someone know she's happy.

As I turn, I take a look at the pile of sheets and towels that still need folding and shove a hand through my tangled mess of hair, now damp and flat against my head.

"I guess we need to finish this up." Quinn opens her eyes first in alarm and then in hesitation as she takes in the pile. "Come on, Quinny girl."

"Don't call me that," she hisses as she walks past me back to her pile, nudging my shoulder a bit aggressively as she passes.

We work together in silence, her holding one edge of the sheet while I hold the other, bringing them together to complete the fold and then repeating it all over again.

I'm not sure how long we work, but by the time we've finished, the sun is hanging high in the sky and we're soaked through as if we've taken a dip in a pool. As we step from the laundry room, we're immediately welcomed by a cool breeze from the air conditioning unit.

"That feels so good," Quinn moans as we make our way back to the check-in desk to let them know we've finished. When we approach, the woman behind the desk gasps in horror at our appearance.

"I am so sorry. It completely slipped my mind that the cool air vent in the laundry room isn't working properly." She rushes out with two bottles of water, handing the first to Quinn.

"It's fine, really. No harm was done. And truthfully it's no different than some of the saunas I've been to. Thank you for the water," Quinn graciously replies as she opens the bottle and brings it to her puckered lips.

"Officer Shaw, is there anything else I can get you or Ms. Miller? We've appreciated all your help today, and I know the group enjoyed the little skit you did earlier."

"I think we're good, Ellen." And then a thought occurs to me and I decide to press my luck a little. "Actually, are Mr. and Mrs. Sampson around? I wanted them to meet Quinn."

I watch as Ellen stutters, knowing full well the type of relationship the Sampsons enjoy, and then I hear Quinn choke on her water.

"Officer Shaw, I don't know if—" Ellen begins but I shake my head, cutting her off as I pat Quinn's back, helping her to catch her breath.

"Don't worry about it. We'll catch them another time. I probably need to get Quinn and Izzy home soon. You let me know if you need anything."

"I will, Officer Shaw. You've been so kind to us."

I nod at Ellen as she takes her place behind the counter once more, then steer Quinn back into the social hall, my hand grazing along her lower back.

"Oh my gosh, what happened to you two?" Izzy cries out as she rushes over and then stops suddenly, her body jerking with the movement. "You both smell."

"Well thanks, sis. We've just spent the past two hours in the laundry room folding linens without any ventilation. It was hot as hell in there."

"Oh, well you still stink. I'm not riding in a car with both of you."

"Hey, Vic," I shout as he finishes a game of checkers with a resident.

"What's up?"

"Can you take Izzy home when you're ready to leave? Quinn and I are going to head out."

"Sure thing, man."

Turning back toward my sister, I say, "Problem solved. We'll meet up for dinner tonight, okay? I'll make a lasagna."

"I would ask where you're going, but I do love your lasagna, so I'm going to keep my mouth shut."

"Good call. Come on, Quinn."

She follows my request wordlessly, but as we step out into the bright sunshine, her hand presses against mine and then her fingers wrap around my palm. I haven't had a woman reach out to hold my hand in years—public displays just aren't my thing—but with Quinn, it feels good, feels right.

Turning my head, I gaze at her, wondering what's going through her mind, but then she drops my hand like it's on fire.

"I'm sorry, that was probably too much. I didn't mean—"

"It's okay, Quinn. I like you holding my hand. You can touch me however you want."

Her radiant smile returns as I grab her hand, clutching it tightly, and it's like a second sun has risen in the sky. Her joy is like the sun bright and overwhelming.

"Do you want to grab some lunch?" I ask just as both of our stomachs growl loudly.

She giggles and she nods enthusiastically. "I thought you'd never ask."

The car comes into view and I guide us toward it, still maintaining the grip of her hand. I let her go to slide into the seat, then rush to the other side of the vehicle and drop down into the seat, immediately starting the car and taking her hand back into mine.

But our reprieve doesn't last long as her phone begins to ring in her bag, which she had tucked into the glove box.

"Sorry," she mouths as she answers the call in a joyful tone that I can tell is as fake as they come.

"Priscilla, I've been waiting for you to call.... Mmhmm."

I try not to eavesdrop on her conversation as I steer the car out into traffic, but in the tight confines of the vehicle, it's difficult.

"The script read-through is going really well. I've had a lot of help," she replies coyly as she peers up at me from beneath her long lashes, then pauses to listen to Priscilla's reply.

"I told you one month. I'll be back before you know it. I bet you already have a brand-new starlet you're pushing to all the casting directors." She looks my way and rolls her eyes.

"Oh," she says then, her tone changing to one of surprise and disappointment. "Well, I guess I could come back a week early, if it's the only time the director could schedule the cast meeting."

Fuck, I only have two and a half more weeks with her? That's not enough time to get her out of my system. It's not enough time to get her out of my head.

At the stoplight, I wait for her eyes to turn toward mine, but they don't. Instead, she wraps an arm around her waist and grips the phone tightly as she begins to talk in more clipped tones until finally she ends the call.

"I'm sorry about that."

"It's okay. So just three weeks now?"

"It seems so. I'm sorry, I didn't plan it this way. I wanted to spend more time with everyone."

"More time with you," I decipher from the look in her eyes.

No feelings, I keep repeating to myself. But in three days it seems we've both dipped our toes into those murky waters. What the hell is going to happen after three weeks? I need to remember that she's leaving, more quickly now than originally planned, and I need to keep my emotions in check. Quinn has no desire to stay here, and I have no desire to change my bachelor ways.

"Izzy is going to be crushed," I hint as I pull through a fried chicken franchise's drive-thru.

She takes a moment to let me order, and as we're waiting in line to pay, she asks almost innocently, "What about you?"

Fixating on her and her mixed expression of despair and hope, I can't bring myself to hurt her, to crush her. Instead, I speak the truth, as much as it pains me.

"I'll be fine, Quinn. I just need to get as much of you as I can while you're here."

Her eyes search mine and I can see my words hurt her more than I intended, but I know she finds the truth in them.

"I'm going to miss you both too, so much. You're the closest thing I have to family."

Our turn to approach the window arrives, and I pay for our lunch and hand the bag to Quinn, which she immediately places on the floor between her legs.

As we start out on the road again, I press, "What about your family, Quinn? Don't you think you should try to see them while you're here? It's been years."

"They don't want to see me."

"I thought they called the other day asking you to stop by for dinner?"

"Yes, they did. But it isn't to see me. It's to chastise me for my choice of career and to tell me how much they wish I'd pursued a career in science like them. I've always disappointed them, and they don't hesitate to tell me so."

"Wow, I had no idea."

"They've never even come out to visit me. Even when I sent them plane tickets and arranged everything. I gave up trying after two years."

"I'm sorry, Quinn. I really am. How about this? I can come with you to the dinner, act as a buffer."

A look of astonishment crosses her face, almost as if the single act of kindness is foreign to her. Surely it can't be. People must clamor to do things for her all of the time.

"You would do that for me?"

"Anything for you, sweetheart."

Silence fills the void in the car, but it's not unpleasant. It's a comfortable mix of two people at ease with themselves and each other.

"When is your next day off or whenever you have an early night?" Quinn asks as she types away on her phone.

Thinking of my schedule, I remember that I'm covering a very early shift on Saturday and that gets me off work at noon.

"I'm free Saturday night if that works for them."

"Don't worry, I'm not giving them a choice," she replies as her fingers move rapidly until she finally tosses the phone back into her bag. She sits back with a huff and crosses her arms.

"Everything okay?" I ask as I approach the worn dirt path off the side of the road and make the sharp right turn.

"Yes, they're just being difficult. Apparently it's a burden to be told when to be available even though they asked. They frustrate me so much. And get this, they really pushed me coming alone, but I said I was bringing a guest whether they liked it or not. So you may have to charm them."

"Don't worry, I can charm anyone. But I'm sure they remember me as a kid."

She laughs loudly, taking me by surprise as she almost curls over from her hysterics. "Don't worry, they barely remember me as a kid and I've known them my whole life. I'm sure you'll have nothing to worry about."

Calming herself down, she finally takes a moment to gaze out of the window and take in her surroundings. "Where are we going?"

"My favorite spot in Dale City." I grin as I steer the car over a few divots in the dirt path. We drive through an open field until we approach a line of trees where I park the car.

I open the door and grab a blanket from the trunk, then make my way over to Quinn's door.

"Come on, it's not far," I tell her as she grips the plastic bag holding our food in one hand and easily slides the other into my open palm.

We walk for a few minutes before she asks, "Do you know where you're going?"

I offer no explanation, just simply confirm that I know where I am and continue walking.

That's when I hear it, the light trickle that will grow in noise the closer we approach. Finally an opening comes into view and I grasp Quinn's hand tighter, excited to share this spot with her. A spot I haven't shared with anyone, not even my twin.

"Is that…?"

"Yep, it's a man-made lake in the middle of nowhere."

I tug her behind me as I make my way toward the lake, aiming for the small sandy beach around the other side.

I inhale the smell of the fresh water and newly cut grass and let my worries wash away. No more work, no more time limit, no more fighting off feelings. Just me and Quinn.

CHAPTER ELEVEN
Quinn

I'M NOT GOING TO lie and say I wasn't worried about where Trevor was carting me off to in the middle of the woods. And then I saw the lake, this beautiful piece of water surrounded by a covering of darkness. It was almost poetic it was so outstanding.

And then Trevor told me this was his spot. His place to wind down, to relax, to just… be. Something I haven't done in more years than I can remember.

"It's gorgeous, Trevor. Thank you so much for bringing me here. I had no idea this even existed."

The blanket slides off his shoulder into his grasp, and he airs it out before laying it on the sandy portion of the ground.

"Most people don't," he confesses. "I had to come out here once a few years back because the owner of the property had found some squatters in an old cabin not far from here. He asked—pleaded, really—for me to patrol the area regularly. And when I agreed, he offered me full access to the lake even though I told him I would've done it regardless."

"That's lovely of you," I declare as I take a seat on the blanket, stretching out my body under the warm Texas sun.

"I felt for him. He had recently lost his wife, and she was the one who had wanted the lake on their property. Apparently, she was a writer and used the cabin as her little writing space when she needed a new perspective. So there was really no way I could turn him down, even if he hadn't offered use of the lake."

He continues divulging about the owner of the property and the stories he was told, and suddenly I feel an overwhelming need to kiss him, to show him how remarkable he is underneath his tough exterior, the one that seems to melt away in my presence.

Tucking my legs under my body, I lean closer to him, cupping his cheeks and pressing my lips to his. No movement or exploration, just my mouth against his, a moment in time captured.

As I pull back, I take a second to take him in: the green flecks in his eyes, the straight nose, straight jaw with just a hint of stubble, and swollen lips. He is the stuff of dreams. I twist so I'm once again facing the lake and extend my legs and feet outward, resting back on my hands.

"Can I ask what that was for?"

"No reason," I reply. "Just felt like it was necessary."

My eyes are closed against the sun as I tilt my head toward the sky, but I hear his distinctive low chuckle.

"Well, feel free to do that anytime you'd like."

"Will do." I smile and turn my face away from the sun's scorching rays, focusing on Trevor instead. "So, ready for lunch?"

He reaches into the plastic bag between us and begins pulling out all of the fixings for a country picnic. Before I know it, I've got a plate full of fried chicken, potato salad, baked beans, and a biscuit situated between my legs.

"So, Quinn, what's it like being a world-famous actress?"

"Oh, so are we doing twenty questions?"

"Naw, just catching up," he clarifies as he folds his empty plate and places it in the plastic bag.

"Do I get to ask you any questions?"

"Sure, but that doesn't mean I'll answer them."

"Fair enough. Let's see, what is it like being a celebrity…."

"World-famous," he chimes in as he opens his bottle of water.

"Yes, world-famous. Sorry. It's great. I mean, I work too much to pay a lot of attention to what goes on around me. My agent keeps me in the know, and my publicist always makes sure I'm in the best light. I do my best to just be me, but LA can be overwhelming, so it's hard not to lose yourself in the glitz and glamour of it all."

"I think you've done pretty well. I'm not going to lie, I don't follow much of what you or any celebrity is up to. I don't have the time. But Izzy and my mom are certainly proud of you."

I haven't been entirely truthful about my life, and I have a sudden urge to disclose it to Trevor.

"Something wrong? You've got this pinched expression on your face like you just ate a lemon."

The end of my braid hangs over my shoulder and I begin absentmindedly twisting it around my fingers

"Nothing's wrong, I just…. Being a celebrity isn't what I signed up for. I just wanted to act. It was my passion, what I was good at. If I only ever got work on a stage, I would be thrilled. And I know I'm far luckier than many of the actors who make their way to Hollywood, don't get me wrong, but being a celebrity is a very intrusive job. There's little to no privacy, and everyone's always out to get something from you. So even though I'm surrounded by people and photographers all day, I've never felt so… lonely."

His eyes take me in, never moving away from my face. I can't see it because my gaze is locked onto the lightly swaying trees just beyond the lake, but I can feel it. I can feel his intensity and protectiveness, and most of all I can feel his pity.

"No friends or boyfriend?"

The heaviness in his voice surprises me, and I find myself training my attention back toward him where he sits with his knees bent and elbows resting atop. He looks so handsome, his pants and polo shirt both tightly pulled against his muscles. I know he normally dresses down when he's away from work, but the fact that he made an effort to dress nicely for the residents at the Dale City Assisted Living Facility makes me even more attracted to him.

"The only person in Hollywood I would call a friend is my agent, Priscilla. As far as boyfriends? I had one a long time ago, but he wasn't too thrilled when my career skyrocketed and he could barely catch a commercial. Typical story. But like I said, it's hard to trust people because you don't know who's out for something else."

Trevor places his hand on top of mine, keeping me from twisting the ends of my hair, then snakes his arm around my shoulders and holds me close, allowing me to soak in his strength.

"I'm sorry, Quinn. So damn sorry," he murmurs into my hair as he presses his mouth to the top of my head.

We sit in silence for a while until it becomes too much.

In jest I lurch away from him, tucking under his arm with a sour expression on my face.

"You really stink."

It takes him a minute, his face pinched until it's clear that my words register. Then he pushes me just enough to almost topple me over.

"I think you're mistaken. You're only smelling yourself."

In mock outrage, I stand up with my hands on my hips. "I do not stink!" I shout.

"You keep telling yourself that, Quinny," he challenges as he stands up, tugging his shirt over his head in the process. I watch in astonishment as his hands move toward the button on his pants, but that's only in the periphery—my eyes are definitely trained on the glistening metal between his nipples.

"What... what are you doing?" I whisper, all of my fake fury brushing away with the breeze.

Tugging his pants down to his ankles, he then toes off his shoes and socks and before fully removing his pants. He stands there in all of his naked glory, and I can't peel my eyes away.

"I'm going for a dip."

"A dip?" I ask in confusion.

"Yes, in the lake. Care to join me?"

Finally tearing my eyes away from his masculine form, I look out onto the cool water of the lake and suddenly yearn to feel it against my skin.

Hesitantly, I question, "Is it safe?" but I already plan on diving in. It looks too divine to turn away from.

"About as safe as I am," Trevor jokes, and then he walks right into the water, about to hip height, before diving under.

I wait for him to emerge, my patience growing thin before he finally does so at the dock in the middle of the lake a moment later.

I grip the edge of my dress but pause. *Should I? Someone could be watching.*

"Come on," he shouts. "Don't be a scaredy-cat."

His taunt does it and I remove my dress with a whirl, tossing it behind me into a heap on the blanket where my panties and bra follow. With a running start, I crash into the calm waters and make it to about waist height before I submerge myself under the cool liquid.

I don't swim far, just enough that I need to tread water, but when I pop back up into the air, I'm surprised to find Trevor wading in front of me.

"There she is."

"This water feels amazing. And there aren't any creepy-crawlies in it."

"Well, I don't know about that, but the owner does have a good filtration system in it because his wife liked to swim, and she too did not like creepy-crawlies."

Something slides across my thigh and I leap into the air practically on top of Trevor, who's laughing raucously.

"You asshole! I thought it was a snake," I cry out as I hold on to him tighter. Luckily he can stand in the spot we're in, just enough to keep his head above the water.

"I couldn't resist."

Now that I have him in close proximity, I take a chance at asking a question that's plagued me for years.

"Hey, Trevor?"

"Hmm?" He swims us out closer to the dock, keeping a tight grip on my waist.

"Why did you leave me?"

My question is met with silence, and for a moment I fear he isn't going to answer, but then his austere voice rings out above the expelling water from his strokes.

"That's a complicated answer. You see, that last night me, you, and Izzy met in the clearing, things were different. I already knew I had a crush on you, but it was the first time I thought that maybe you had one too."

"You had a crush on me?"

"Shh."

"Sorry, I just never knew."

"Anyway, I thought that would be it, that the night in the clearing would be my chance to make my move. But I noticed Izzy was acting strangely. Well, stranger than she normally did, so I held back. It seemed like she needed you.

"When I asked her about it the next day while we were all recovering from those hangovers, she said she had overheard Mom and Dad talking about an anniversary of a miscarriage from a few years after we were born. Apparently, my mom was pregnant with an unexpected baby, and she lost it. Izzy had wanted a sibling other than me for as long as I can remember, which was why she was so excited when you moved across the street. So I knew I had to keep my distance from you. You were the closest thing to a sister she was ever going to get, and I couldn't take that from her."

I wade in the water, contemplating his words. It makes sense now, why Izzy pushed me that night about not having a crush on her brother, why she pushes it now.

"So, what's changed?" I ask.

"What do you mean?"

"Why is now any different?"

"Because we're different. Because the situation is different. Because I want to know what it feels like to have you."

"Do you have me?" I whisper.

Trevor's lips brush against mine and I'm lost for a moment until he says, "I have you until you decide you don't want me anymore."

I don't need much buildup as Trevor eases himself into me. Our bodies are in sync enough that the delicious friction has us plummeting over the edge quickly.

From our stakeout on the dock, we dry under the sun, both of us baring our bodies to the heat. We speak about nothing and everything, just about our lives. The trivial things that don't matter to anyone else but ourselves. I learn that he loves Chinese food and late-night movies, and he hasn't taken a vacation since he graduated high school and his parents took him and Izzy to the Bahamas. I also learned that they had booked a ticket for me as well, but I had stubbornly left with a quick "good riddance."

Trevor keeps a tight grasp on my hand, almost as if he's afraid I'll slip away, but it's fine with me because the touch of his hand against my palm makes me feel complete.

The sun begins to drop behind the tree line, and we begrudgingly make our way back to the beach in the heated water. I feel like we're out of our own cocoon and into a world separate from our own.

As we tug on our clothes, Trevor mentions having to go to the store to grab items for the lasagna, and I offer to tag along.

Now that my time with him has been cut short, I want to be as close to him as possible—feelings be damned.

RENEE HARLESS

CHAPTER TWELVE
Trevor

*W*HAT HAD BEEN A great afternoon with Quinn on Wednesday turned into a nightmare when Izzy questioned why we arrived home after her. We didn't lie, but we only told her about the picnic at the lake, not what happened in the water. That would've scarred her for life. Instead, we ate an awkward meal, and I had to leave Quinn without so much as a kiss on the cheek.

I haven't seen her for two days, both due to my schedule and Izzy. I'm fearful of crossing that line again because I know how much Quinn means to my sister. She isn't just her best friend, she's the sister Izzy always wanted.

I've been craving her, still crave her, and the only release I've been able to find is with my own palm or a workout in my home gym. I've worked out so much in the last two days that every muscle in my body aches.

The clock on my computer finally switches from 11:59 a.m. to 12:00 p.m., and I hurriedly grab my bag and make my way out of the station.

Once I step foot in my door, I send a message to Quinn letting her know I'm home and to text me when she wants me to pick her up.

Hoping the answer is sooner rather than later, I divulge myself of my clothes and quickly jump into the shower. Normally I'll spend a few good minutes underneath the warm spray, letting the rivulets cleanse me, but today I'm hurried because I'm beyond anxious to see Quinn.

With the towel wrapped firmly around my waist, I exit my master bath only to stop suddenly with my mouth hanging agape.

"You're going to catch flies like that," my sweet southern belle laughs as she sits primly on the corner of my bed.

"Quinn, I—what are you doing here?"

"I…." She hesitates as she glances down at her hands twisting in her lap.

Meandering slowly toward her, I stop just beyond her knees. She must notice my towel in her line of sight because she tilts her head back to gaze up at me.

"You what, sweetheart?"

"I just missed you, that's all."

I tug her legs toward my body, knocking her back onto the bed, her hair spreads around her face like a golden halo.

"You are so beautiful," I whisper.

"Kiss me, Trevor."

Swooping in, I merge our mouths together, licking and sucking at her lips until she begins to rock her hips against the softness of my towel. My back arches as I bend over her, sliding my knee between the apex of her thighs. It's been so long since I've seen her that I can feel the vein in my cock pulsating as blood surges toward my erection.

Quinn's slender fingers reach for the knot in my towel at the same time I hear a single knock and then the front door to my house open. I push myself away from Quinn reluctantly and stand in front of my dresser in hopes to hide the obvious tent beneath the towel.

"Hey, Trevor," I hear Izzy shout as she comes up the stairs. Quinn scrambles to find someplace to go, but she's too late and just settles back on the bed. "Can I borrow the keys—what's going on?"

Quinn's face pales in horror, but luckily nothing on her is out of place, not even a single wave in her hair.

"Hey, sis. Quinn asked me to go with her to her parents' house tonight to help diffuse any problems at dinner. She was just stopping by to ask, but she caught me while I was in the shower."

"I don't believe you," Izzy firmly declares as she crosses her arms over her chest.

"It's true, Iz," Quinn jumps in. "You're going on that date with Vic tonight, and I just knew I'd need someone to come with me. You know I hate dinners with my parents."

"Then why are you still in a towel, T?"

I roll my eyes. "Because I just got out of the shower, Iz, like literally a minute before you walked in. I was grabbing clothes to go change, and then I was coming right back out. Calm down or you're going to get wrinkles."

"I am not!" she shouts, then shakily puts her hand to her head and rushes into the bathroom to check for any crevices in her skin.

"You okay?" I mouth to Quinn, who shrugs indifferently.

Izzy comes back into the room and snarls at me like a rabid dog.

"I hate you sometimes."

"No you don't. Now, what is it you want?"

"For you to put clothes on."

"Iz!"

"Fine, I was going to ask if I could borrow the keys to the Shelby."

My back stiffens as she asks to take out my restored 1965 Shelby Mustang. Izzy isn't known to be the most cautious behind the wheel, and I can just imagine my baby wrapped around some tree at her expense.

"I'm not sure, Iz."

"What if I let Vic drive? He wants to go to Houston tonight, and it's so gorgeous outside."

Maybe if I let her use the car she'll forget about what she almost walked in on moments ago. Hopefully.

"All right, Iz. But only if Vic drives it, understand?"

"Yes, two-minute-older brother, I promise. You're the best."

"I know." I slip the key ring into her waiting grasp. "Take good care of her," I implore as she twirls on her heels and exits the room.

She pauses at the top of the steps and peers into the bedroom, only gazing at me.

"You too, Trevor."

Back in the room, I'm greeted with silence. Quinn is now standing awkwardly next to my king-size bed, her face carrying the weight of a thousand mistakes.

"I shouldn't have come here. I'm sorry."

Having shoved my legs into a pair of dark jeans, I let them hang loosely around my hips as I stalk toward Quinn, my bare feet slapping across the hardwood until they meet the soft fibers of the rug.

"I'm glad you did."

"But now Izzy's on alert. I think she suspects something, Trevor."

"Probably."

"Trevor!"

Taking her hand in mine, I rub the soft knuckles on top, the movement instantly relaxing her.

"Sweetheart, look. We both know Izzy isn't stupid. She's trying to piece things together that she suspected while we were in school. But she also isn't going to say anything unless she has hardcore evidence. She doesn't like confrontation."

Her chest rises and falls as she takes a shuddering breath and then steps into my arms, pressing her warm cheek against my bare chest.

"I can't lose her as a friend," Quinn sighs into my chest, and I instinctively place my hand on the back of her head, holding her closer to me.

"You won't lose her as a friend. I'll make sure of it."

Even if that means having to walk away.

"Come on." I step away, instantly missing the heat from her body pressed against mine. "I believe we have a few hours to kill until we're needed at dinner."

Quinn nods silently and then moves toward my bedroom door.

"I'm just... going to wait for you downstairs."

"Are you sure? I'll be just a minute."

"Yeah. Yeah, I'm sure."

I watch her retreating back head down the stairs and then shake the unsettling feeling in my chest. I have to keep reminding myself that there are no feelings. It's the only way to keep it simple and uncomplicated. But fuck, if her broken face doesn't pierce something inside of me.

I quickly throw on a henley T-shirt that fits a bit snug against my arms and chest. Quinn said the dinner was informal, so I don't grab a button-down shirt though a part of me still thinks I should, just in case. It's hot and humid out today, and I wish I could just toss on a pair of shorts, but I want to look like I made some sort of effort for her parents. Sliding my feet into a pair of running shoes, I glide down the steps and search for Quinn.

She isn't in the living room or the kitchen. In a bit of panic, I start to scramble around my house, afraid she's deserted me, deserted us. My shoes skid across the hardwood floor as my dread rises, filling my stomach with fear. Suddenly I hear a squeaking coming from outside and I rush toward my front door.

My beautiful girl sits on the porch swing, one leg tucked under the other while the toe of her boot rests on the wood of the porch, rocking her back and forth. Her golden hair drapes over her shoulder in silky waves as she lays her head along the top of the bench, peering out over my front yard.

I take a moment to take her in before I break her peacefulness. The screen door thumps behind me, and Quinn flinches slightly, but her body doesn't move from its position.

"I wondered where you went."

"Sorry. It's such a lovely day out, and with the fan overhead it's just perfect."

The pull of her closeness is too overwhelming and I find myself mindlessly drifting toward her, taking the seat beside her on the swing. She immediately begins to reposition her head and legs, but I throw my arm on the back of the bench and push her head back down onto my shoulder. It's faint but I can hear her sigh of contentment as I begin to rock the swing with my feet, allowing her to pull her other leg up onto the bench.

The breeze from the overhead fan keeps the Texas heat at bay and I fall into a deep relaxation, the first I've had in years. My fingers absentmindedly drag up and down Quinn's smooth arms, and I smirk when a shiver shakes her body.

I can't help but feel that this moment, this feeling, is perfect.

"What if your sister sees us?" Quinn implores in a voice rough with pleasure, and then I realize that I spoke my thoughts out loud.

Tilting my head, I peer down into Quinn's hesitant brown eyes, alarm and shame churning in them.

I slide my hand into her hair, gripping the strands harshly, and bring her head toward me.

"Don't care," I murmur against her lips as I meld them with mine. It takes a bit of persistence, but she finally relaxes and opens herself to me. My tongue explores the far reaches of her mouth, her own sliding against mine with every pass. Her taste is addictive, exotic, and I want more, so much more. For a moment I forget where we are, rocking back and forth on my porch swing for anyone to see, and grip Quinn's waist and tug her onto my lap. Instantly I feel her heat between her legs through the thick denim of my jeans and my arousal stiffens. With my hands planted firmly on her hips, I rock her against my erection and capture her moan in my mouth.

"Trevor," she says between kisses. "We need to stop."

I have little strength to halt my movements; she feels too good against me.

Shakily, she appeals again, and I find the power to pull back from her sweet taste.

Her eyes remain closed as I stare, memorizing her beautiful features. To most, her ivory skin, wide brown eyes, plump lips, and button nose make her attractive. But to me, it's the innocence of her gaze, the way her mouth curves subtly as if she always has a small smile in place, and the softness of her cheeks.

She's not beautiful because she's a world-famous actress. She's beautiful because she's little Quinn Miller who moved across the street when we were thirteen. She's beautiful because she followed her dreams and made something of herself. She's beautiful because even if I never have another chance to have her in my arms, I'll remember every detail of how it felt to have her for just a moment, just a dash of our lifetime, and she let me have that chance.

"What has you thinking so hard?" she asks, and I realize I've been staring at her while thoughts cascade through my mind.

"Just lost in thought. And I'm sorry I took this too far," I apologize as I move her off my lap, instantly missing her warmth, even in this ridiculous heat.

"That's okay, I liked it. And I don't think anyone saw anything."

The swing starts rocking again as I kick us off with the tip of my shoe.

"So, anything you want to do to kill time?"

Her cheeks redden and I immediately realize that she's thinking of us heading back up to my bedroom. Something I'm not opposed to, but I don't want our entire time together to be about sex, even though it is incredible. Quinn was my friend far before we took it to this step, and I want to prove to her that we can be friends when everything is said and done.

"Have you been downtown yet? We have a couple new shops."

"Oh, no I haven't. I'd like to see how things have changed. It sounds fun. I haven't eaten lunch yet either. Is Erma's Sandwich Shop still around? I could go for one of her Italian subs and a frozen lemonade."

"Erma's is still alive and kicking. Best sandwiches in all of Houston sixty years running."

Quinn jumps from the swing and I follow dutifully, knowing I'd follow her anywhere right now as her hips sway with each step, her dress brushing against the back of her thighs, teasing me.

I settle her in my car and then do the same, starting the ignition and looking out onto the street.

"Come on, let's go eat!" she joyfully exclaims, and I trail my gaze from her legs up her body. It only takes a moment for her to realize what I took from her comment.

"Trevor, I meant sandwiches."

"But you're my favorite meal."

She giggles as if she doesn't believe me, but she's totally wrong. I would devour her for every meal if she'd let me.

*

AN HOUR LATER, QUINN and I are walking down the sidewalk under the green awnings synonymous with Dale City, each with a frozen lemonade in hand. The summer heat squelches, but the refreshing drink keeps us cool. I love watching Quinn's cheeks hollow out as she sips from the straw between her pink-tinted lips. The action reminds me of the way she sucked my cock the other day in the laundry room. And as if my most treasured asset senses my thoughts, it begins to grow behind my pants, achingly pressing against the zipper of my jeans.

With my mind elsewhere, I don't notice the buxom woman heading in our direction, or the venom spilling from her eyes toward Quinn, or the stroller she's pushing irritably toward us. In her stacked heels, Mindy Caldwell hobbles over with fire in her eyes. Unfortunately, Mindy was a menace in high school, and it looks like she's itching for a repeat performance. Though she's *Playboy*-pinup gorgeous, she hides behind her silicone-filled body and has a mean streak to rival anyone else in Houston.

As she approaches, her puckered mouth grows into an overly fake smile, her bright white, straight teeth on display. And in horror, her eyes narrow in on my hand clasped with Quinn's, something that innocently occurred as we left the shop but now seems as if it's going to cause trouble.

"Well, Officer Shaw, what a pleasure it is to see you," she purrs as she closes in. Quinn squeezes my hand tightly and I look over to see her face blanched. Then I remember how Mindy and her minions teased and tortured, for all intents and purposes, Quinn in high school. If it hadn't been for my sister, I'm sure it all would've been much worse, but Izzy was the head cheerleader and one of the most popular girls in our school; you didn't mess with her or Quinn and not get some sort of retribution.

"I wish I could say the same, Mindy. Of course, you remember Quinn Miller, right?"

Mindy's nose bunches as if she's smelled something foul as her eyes travel up and down Quinn's body.

"Yes, how could I forget little Quinn? What have you been up to?"

"Mindy," I press. "You don't live under a rock. You know Quinn has made something of herself. How lucky are we here in Dale City to have an actress of her caliber in our midst?"

"I'm not sure I would consider acting a job. I mean, how hard can it be?" she accuses.

Quinn takes a sip of her drink and then asks, "So, what is it you do, Mindy? If I remember correctly, you wanted to be a fashion designer one day."

It's difficult but I hold back my laugh as Mindy's eyes narrow and her nostrils flare.

"I'm a stay-at-home mom."

"That's wonderful! I know it can't be easy. How many children do you have?" Quinn leans over to peer into the stroller.

"Just the one," Mindy barks and then softens as she looks back at me. "Officer Shaw, would you like to look at your baby?"

My eyes narrow into thin slits at Mindy's implied meaning. We've never slept together, though she tried for years.

"Yours?" Quinn asks as she coughs on her lemonade.

"No, not mine," I reply harshly, my angered gaze still on Mindy as she smiles without a care in the world. "Little Billy Jr. belongs to Billy Smithson. You probably remember him from school. I helped deliver Billy Jr. when Mindy's water broke at the supermarket."

"Oh, that's Billy now," Mindy hums as she waves across the street to the ex-quarterback with a growing tire around his waist.

Quinn's expression is masked by her curiosity of the baby cooing at her from the stroller.

"Sorry about her," I whisper to Quinn, who peeks at me from behind her long lashes and shoots me a quick smile before putting her attention back on the baby.

"Billy, Mindy, it was a pleasure to see you as always," I lie. "Quinn and I have some plans, but I'm sure I'll be seeing you all later."

Quinn stands and takes my hand in hers as if it's as natural as flowers blooming in spring.

"Good to see you, Mindy," Quinn echoes as we walk past her nemesis.

I watch in amazement as the woman walking beside me takes a sip of her drink as if we hadn't just spent the past five minutes reopening old scars left by our pasts. Needing her closer, I release her hand and wrap my arm around her shoulders, kissing the top of her head. Her arm wedged between our bodies wraps around my waist, and I wish it was a permanent fixture holding me to her.

We pass by a sprouting of bushes blocking a parking lot from the buildings, and I turn Quinn toward me and kiss her for everything she's worth.

RENEE HARLESS

THE RULE BREAKER 175

CHAPTER THIRTEEN
Trevor

*T*HE HOUSE SITS IN the middle of the same two-acre lot it's occupied since before I was born. My parents still live across the street, but when Quinn moved away, I had a hard time gazing at the home that seemed more foreign to me than ever before.

The two-story brick colonial is large, mimicking a few of the other houses on the street, but strangely it always seemed a bit dark to me. Shadows linger on its surface from the surrounding trees, but it's the shadows on the inside that intrigue me most. It's still hard to this day to picture bright and bubbly Quinn living in a house that's her opposite.

RENEE HARLESS

Growing up, we never saw her parents much. Just comings and goings from work, leaving Quinn alone in the massive estate, far too big for a teenager, which is why she spent many nights sleeping over with Izzy. My parents love Quinn, but the same can't be said for her parents toward me and my sister. They always complained when we were over and would send us home claiming Quinn needed to spend her time studying. Except that was typically what we were doing.

I remember how hard her parents pushed her in school, but they never made an effort to support her. Izzy and I never saw them at any of Quinn's plays or her high school graduation. She didn't even get to go to prom because her parents were taking her to a medical convention across the country. That part had hurt me just as much as it had hurt her. I had plans to ask her to senior prom, even turned down requests from some of the most popular girls in our school. I had my sights set on only one girl, and that girl was Quinn. When I found out she wasn't able to go, I begged my parents to see if she could stay with us, but they said it wasn't up to them and I needed to find someone else to take. My heart had hurt for her, so I had no qualms about the fact that she up and left after graduation.

So as I pull into the driveway with the murky darkness closing in on the car, my past anger and hurt for Quinn boils at the surface, threatening to overflow.

"Quinn," I start as I turn off the car and twist in my seat to face her, "if I say anything out of line tonight, I want to go ahead and apologize now."

"What do you mean?"

"Well, I just…." I run a hand through my hair as I try to find the words expressing my feelings toward her parents. "I just want to protect you, and if they say anything condescending, I'll probably snap."

She rests her small hand against my cheek, and I want to lean into her touch more than anything right now. Strangely enough, it's as if she's comforting me and not the other way around.

"Trevor, you don't have to stand up for me. I'm a big girl."

"I know I don't have to, but I want to. My job is to serve and protect, remember?"

"Ah, yes. Officer Shaw. How different our lives turned out to be."

"I want to kiss you now, Quinn."

Her brown eyes dart toward the front door but quickly come back to me.

"Okay," she whispers and I swoop in, craving her lips against mine.

I forget about the house before us, my parents' house across the street, or the fact that we live in two different worlds. For this moment she's mine, and I'm making it count.

Ten minutes later, we enter the house behind Quinn's scowling mother. I used to wonder how it would feel to awkwardly walk into a house where you weren't wanted, and boy, it is not a good feeling.

The interior looks the same as it did when Quinn lived here; not much has changed in the six years since she left. I almost feel sad for her parents until they move into the dining room without a greeting and begin saying a prayer at the table before Quinn and I have even taken a seat ourselves.

With a shrug, Quinn asks what I would like to drink and then steps into the kitchen to fill two glasses with water. We move into the dining room where her parents are divvying up the meal onto plates between the two of them. The lasagna does smell delicious, so I scoop a square onto my plate and repeat the same for Quinn, who takes a seat beside me instead of next to her mother.

Silence builds and grows and festers until it's tearing at the seams. The scrape of our utensils and chewing from her father are the only sounds in the room until a throat clearing calls from across the table.

"Quinn, when were you going to tell us that you were in town visiting?" her mother inquires.

"I'm supposed to be reviewing the script for my next movie. And I'm already having to go back early. And truthfully, I didn't think you wanted to see me."

Fascinated, I listen as her mother ignores the quip about not wanting to be seen and focuses on the script.

"Are you still doing the acting thing?" she asks disdainfully, and I'm surprised that she doesn't seem to realize how successful her daughter is in the industry.

"Mother, please," Quinn pleads as she looks over at me, embarrassment coloring her cheeks.

"I'm surprised to see you, Trevor. Isn't there some vagrant you should be arresting?"

"Mother!" Quinn cries before I have a chance to retaliate.

"I'm sorry, but what is so wrong with being an officer of the law?" I question.

"Nothing, other than it takes no real formal education. Pass a mental and physical test and you're in. And we all know both of those can be stretched," her father chimes in, and I begin to see red.

Who do these people think they are?

"Well, I'll be sure to remember the next time one of those vagrants needs medical care and has to be restrained and monitored at the hospital that it takes very little mental and physical strength."

"Trevor," Quinn shushes, and I refrain from saying any more, as vile as her parents seem to be at the moment. "Mother, is there a particular reason why you requested my presence tonight?"

"Is it not enough that I want to see my child?"

Quinn sits patiently, knowing her parents have a reason or they wouldn't have requested her to visit at all.

"Okay, Quinn, have it your way. We've asked you to come because your father and I are moving. We need you to take your things and clean out your room."

Not so bad. Them moving isn't the end of the world, but my mouth goes dry as they slide a set of thick papers across the table.

"What's this?" Quinn asks as she grasps the stack.

"Your adoption papers," her mother mentions casually, as if this information isn't life-destroying for their daughter.

Quinn has tears in her eyes as she asks, "My... my what?"

"You're adopted, Quinn," her father says stoically as he takes a sip from his drink.

"Er, excuse me," Quinn murmurs as she rushes from the table, her hand pressed to her mouth.

I want to go after her, my body pleading with me to rise from the table and hurry behind her, but my heart aches for Quinn. Her parents continue eating as if they haven't just devastated her, haven't just pulled the rug out from under everything she's ever known, haven't destroyed the heart that beats inside her.

"How could you?" I demand without remorse as my fury triggers something deep inside. "How could you do this to her in that way?"

"She should know."

"Sure she should, but not like this. Don't you love her at all? Can't you see this will tear her apart? I don't even understand how you could've adopted her."

"I was working on a surgery for a drug-addicted patient who came in after being shot. The patient died on the table, but we were able to save the baby. I knew I was up as a candidate for the chief of surgery at the hospital we were working at, and at the time it was very family-centric. It wasn't enough that I was married. As a woman, I needed to have children."

"So you stole her?" my officer instincts solicit.

"No, we simply requested to adopt her. We were in good standings with social services, and they let us take her home three weeks later."

"Did you get the job?"

"Of course I got the job. After everything was said and done, I wasn't quite sure what to do with the baby once I was promoted, so we kept her instead of putting her back into the system."

"How kind of you," I say icily.

"Not that it needs any explanation, but our jobs were too hectic to take the time to have children the natural way. This worked in our favor. We had only hoped that she would follow in our footsteps. Instead, we were stuck with a child who had dreams of her name in lights."

"Do you have any idea how successful your daughter is? How remarkable she is at her craft?"

"We don't follow entertainment. It's too barbaric and brain-numbing. I'm sure she's successful enough."

"Well, I'll have you know that your daughter is one of the most sought-after actresses in the world. She's been nominated for numerous awards and won a few."

"But has she won them all?"

Rage fills my bones and wrath ignites in my veins, causing me to lash out.

"Are you kidding me right now?" I stand and slam my fists onto the table, ignoring the pain from the hard surface. "I can't even do this right now. How dare you demean your own daughter like this. She is remarkable, and you're missing an opportunity to support her in a way that all parents should. Shame on you. I'll be taking your daughter away from here, and I hope to never hear from you again."

"What about her things? We need them gone," her mother adds as if it's an inconvenience.

"I'm sure you can manage to hire someone to pack it all up, and you can give it to my parents. We'll make sure she gets her things."

Without a second thought, I force myself away from the dining room and go after Quinn. Luckily I don't have to search far, because I find her standing just inside the kitchen in hearing range of our conversation. Her tears have dried up, only small black smudges evident under her eyes, but the look of rage in them has me taking a step back.

She bypasses me and storms over to the table guns blaring, slamming her fists onto the table across from her mother.

"How could you? All these years I've spent berating myself for not being good enough, for not being the daughter you wished I could be. And to find out after all this time that I was never your daughter to begin with? Did you even love me?"

"Quinn, don't be so dramatic," her mother sighs as she takes a sip of her water, and I watch as the fire in Quinn's eyes flares to enormous heights.

"Dramatic? You're saying that *I'm* being dramatic? I just found out I was adopted by two people only hoping to get a heads-up in their careers, and you do it in front of my guest."

"Yes, you're being dramatic. It's just some papers."

"It's my fucking life!" she shouts and then breathes heavily as she tries to calm herself down. "All of my life I've wondered what I could've done to make you both hate me so much. How you could look at me like I was just a plant you kept around to feed and water when the time suited you. Well, now I know why," she says in an eerily calm voice before she stands straight and looks over at me.

We don't exchange words; instead, I wrap my arm around her and escort her out of the house.

"Quinn," I prod as I start the car, hoping to get her attention.

"Hmm?"

"What do you want? What do you need?"

She remains taciturn, her voice vanishing after learning what she has this evening.

"Do you want me to get Izzy?"

Her soft waves move as she shakes her head back and forth.

"I want to help you, sweetheart. What can I do to help you?" I urge as I rest my hand on her cheek, hoping to soothe her with my touch. Her body relaxes slightly, but I can tell she's still wound tight, and my own heart is breaking inside of my chest.

"Trevor?"

"Yes?"

"Take me back to your place."

CHAPTER FOURTEEN
Quinn

I AM POSSESSED. A lost figure in the black abyss of life, and I have no real destination for solace. All I want, all I crave, is the feel of Trevor. Something warm, something solid, something real. And I need it more than my next breath.

When Trevor asked me what I needed, where I wanted to go, I could only think of one place where I felt secure—and that was with him. I didn't hesitate when I told him to take me to his house. I want to be completely encapsulated by him, feel like a part of him.

The temptation he holds is overwhelming, and I know at this point my feelings are beginning to blossom, regardless of how many pep talks I've had with myself to keep things buried deep. The challenge now will be not letting Trevor figure out that I'm falling for him so much more than I did when I was younger. Our quick and easy sexcapade is getting muddled in a swamp of emotions that I don't know how to navigate through.

Luckily as we pull into Trevor's driveway, he takes the lead knowing I'm on the verge of some cataclysmic breakdown. Reaching over, he unclasps my seat belt and then exits the car, quickly coming around the other side to escort me out.

As he guides me into his house, the feeling in the room begins to shift as he takes my hand. I trail behind him as we move into his kitchen, where Trevor turns around and rests his hands on my hips. I almost think he's going to bend down and kiss me as he stares into my eyes, but instead I find myself lifted into the air and plopped onto the counter.

He walks toward the sink, reaches into the cabinet to grab a glass, and then fills it with water.

"Drink," he commands gently as he holds it out to me.

I take it with a shaky hand and drink the full glass in one sitting and hand it back to Trevor, who deposits it in the sink. Like a ghost, he floats toward me and scoops me into his arms, settling me tight against his chest before he takes the steps two at a time.

Trevor opens his bedroom door with a squeak, and as he stalks toward the massive bed, a shiver snakes down my spine.

"Cold?" he asks, but I shake my head.

I'm heated through to my core right now.

Gently Trevor sets me on the bed and tugs on my skirt, silently asking whether I want it removed or not. And I do, I want to rid myself of everything that reminds me of tonight. Seeming to know what I need, Trevor glides the dress from my body, lifting it over my head and tossing it aimlessly into the room. Reaching around, he unclasps my bra and it joins my dress on the floor.

I close my eyes as I anticipate his touch, but I'm surprised when I'm lifted into his arms again. Before I can figure out what's going on, I'm lying on the bed and Trevor is wrapping the covers around me.

"What's going on?"

"You need to rest, Quinn. You just learned some pretty big news."

"But I... I need you more, Trevor," I whisper as I hunker down under the warm soft duvet.

He contemplates my words and emotion as he takes me in, and I feel helpless in his gaze.

"How about I lie with you? I need to get you back home before my sister returns."

"You could just say we're practicing the script."

As he moves to the other side of the bed and slides beneath the sheets, his frown tilts down farther.

"I'm not a fan of lying."

"We're lying every day when we hide whatever it is we're doing from her," I explain as I turn over and watch him.

"I know."

A few minutes of quiet pass, neither of us doing much but breathing. I watch his chest rise and fall as he lies on his back. Taking a chance, I scoot closer to him and rest my cheek on his chest, loving the way I can hear his heart beat against my ear.

"Do you want to talk about it, Quinn?"

"I guess. It really explains why they treated me the way they did. I'm not even sure if I'm upset, I'm just... nothing. Hollow. Like I found out that this part of me I'd been trying to fit into a hole was a square peg all along."

"Quinn, no one deserved to be treated the way you have, adopted or not."

"Adopted." My voice shakes as the realization finally hits. "I'm adopted, Trevor."

The sobs break free and I become a shell of myself as I fall apart in Trevor's arms. He doesn't seem to mind my breakdown, not caring that I'm leaving a trail of tears down his chest. Instead, he holds me close and wraps me in his arms, soothing me with his embrace.

It takes a while but I find myself drying up, not enough tears left to shed over the news I received from my so-called parents. The parents who barely paid me any mind while I lived under their roof. It explains their treatment and why they didn't seem too bothered when I left. Except now I have absolutely nothing tying me to Dale City.

As the fear begins to well deep inside, harnessing my insecurities, I close my eyes and relish in the moment of being in Trevor's arms—for however long it lasts. His fingers trace up and down my bare back, following the path of my spine, and it calms my thoughts.

Before I know it I'm drifting away toward sleep, letting the blackness pull me in.

The slamming of the front door wakes me up and I quickly realize I'm no longer resting on Trevor's chest but his sheets instead. Turning my head, I notice the remaining half of the bed is empty as well.

I can make out harsh whispers coming from the bottom of the stairs, and I recognize Izzy's voice.

"What's going on, Trevor?"

"Izzy, it's not what it seems. I'm just lying here on the couch while she's sleeping upstairs. There's nothing going on. My God, Iz, she just had her world torn apart."

"What happened? I got your message, but it just said Quinn learned some terrible news tonight," Izzy whispers, but I can't listen to Trevor's reply. It makes it real then. If the words are in my head, I can push them away and pretend none of this happened.

I place the pillow over my head and tune them out, mentally reading the script for my latest movie to drown out my thoughts.

A knock on the door sounds a few minutes later, and Trevor enters the room with a sullen expression on his face. His typically dreamy eyes are heavy with sympathy and concern, and truthfully I don't like it one bit.

"Izzy is probably going to want to spend the day with you tomorrow."

"How'd she take it?"

"I figured you were awake. She took it okay. She's worried about you. She's afraid you're going to push away all your feelings until it becomes too much." Trevor walks closer to the bed, his bare chest highlighted by the low-slung gray sweatpants. With each step, I can make out his cock swinging freely between his legs, and heat builds in my center.

"Quinn?" he asks, but my train of thought was elsewhere so I hum, hoping he'll repeat himself. "Quinn, are you going to be okay? Is it too much right now? I can back off. We can just do the friend thing for the rest of your time here."

"Don't you dare. The sex with you is about the only thing in my life that I know and have control of. I... I'm not sure I could handle anything else right now."

Sighing, Trevor takes a seat on the bed and exhales. "Quinn, you will always have me and Izzy. You can count on us for anything, you know that, right?"

"I know." I sit up in bed and wrap my arms around myself protectively. "So what happens now?" I ask as I look over at him.

"Well, what do you say we watch a movie in bed? I have to be at work at six in the morning, but I told Izzy I was keeping you here since you were resting, and I was staying on the couch."

"I don't care what we watch, but I'd like to lie with you."

Trevor grabs his remote and turns on the television mounted on the wall across from the bed, selecting a movie already playing on a station. A few cars move quickly across the screen as he saunters back toward the bed, tucking himself under the sheets.

He rolls me onto my side and he does the same, his chest to my back, and props his head on his bent arm to watch the movie over my shoulder. I last about twenty minutes before the feeling of his thick cock pressing against my bottom becomes too much. Being aroused when Trevor is around has been a daily occurrence since

I've returned home, so my sex is already wet and aching for him.

Yearning to feel his closeness, I slowly guide my hand across my hips and behind my body. When I'm met with the soft waistband of his sweats, I snake my hand underneath the elastic and gently caress the head of his cock.

"What are you doing, sweetheart?" he asks as he presses a kiss to my shoulder, a growl sounding deep in his chest as I stroke his shaft from base to tip.

"I'm thanking you for taking care of me tonight." I squeeze him just enough to trigger another growl, and I smile victoriously.

"You don't need to thank me," Trevor says through gritted teeth.

Instantly I stop my movements and peer at him from over my shoulder. "Do you want me to stop?"

"Fuck no, I just want you to know that I'm not expecting this. That I care about you too much to have sex with you tonight."

Saucily I stroke his hardened shaft once more, loving the way the velvet skin feels against my palm, and admire the way his body shivers with the movement. Jokingly, I ask, "Are those feelings, Trevor?"

As if something inside him snaps, he tugs me over so I'm straddling his hips and rocks himself against my apex, coating his sweat pants in my heat.

"If you want me, Quinn, you take what you need."

I tug down his pants and use my feet to push them down to his ankles, enthralled by the look of fascination on Trevor's face. His arms rest behind his head in a relaxing manner, but I know it's to keep himself from reaching out and taking control.

I guide him into my sheath and slip him in inch by inch until I'm completely seated and full. Trevor bites his lower lip as I rock against him, craving the sensation as he hits my sensitive spot.

The feeling is incredible and I try to hold back, try to savor it all, but the impulse to take everything becomes too great. As if he senses my desire, Trevor says, "Take it, Quinn."

And with his permission, I lose control.

A small lamp automatically turns on in the corner, and I realize it must still be early since darkness looms out the window. From where I rest on my stomach, barely covered by a sheet, I watch as Trevor pulls on his standard-issue navy pants and a button-down shirt. He grabs his badge and gun from his dresser and straps them onto his person before turning in my direction.

"Good morning, beautiful." He smiles as he leans down and kisses me tenderly.

"Hey, I guess I should get going too." Sitting up, I yawn and stretch my arms only to find Trevor's gaze homed in on my exposed breasts. Normally I'd have the urge to cover them up, but not with Trevor. The way he's looking at me makes me feel irresistible.

"No, you stay put and catch a few more hours of sleep. Izzy knows where you are."

Slinking back against the bed and tugging the covers over my body, I smile up at him.

"I wish I could stay in bed with you all day." He gazes down at me, his eyes filled with sincerity and desire.

"Maybe one day soon?"

"Maybe," he says as the alarm sounds on the phone in his pocket. "Whelp, I need to run. I'm on call for the next three days, but we can do some read-throughs at night if you're open to it."

"I don't have any plans."

"And Wednesday I'd like to take you out."

My heart starts pounding in my chest at the thrill of his request.

"Like a date?"

Trevor falters and my hopes nose-dive as his expression changes.

"I mean, maybe? Yeah, it can be a date."

"Trevor, you don't have to do me any favors. I remember it's just sex," I lash out.

Unexpectedly, he places a knee on the bed and leans over, sealing his mouth against mine. "I'm taking you on a date because I want to, not because I have to. I just haven't taken anyone on a date in a very long time."

"Oh."

"Yeah, oh. Now get some rest, sweetheart. Hopefully I'll see you tonight."

I watch as his tight ass moves with each step toward his door.

"Hey, Trevor," I shout to get his attention before he descends the staircase. "Thank you, for last night. I… I needed that."

"I'm yours whenever you need me," he replies before he disappears from my view.

As I sink farther down into the sheets, worry begins to build that soon I might need him more than ever.

RENEE HARLESS

CHAPTER FIFTEEN
Quinn

RIFLING THROUGH MY STASH of clothes, I anxiously pull out a pair of distressed jean shorts and a loose-fitted T-shirt. Yesterday when I asked Trevor where we were heading tonight, he said just to dress casually; I sure as hell hope this is what he means.

The front door closes and I assume it's Izzy letting Vic into her place. After I woke from Trevor's on Sunday and did a self-inflicted walk of shame back to Izzy's house, we spent the day together on her back porch sipping mimosas. It was everything I had imagined our time together to be: a little bit of gossip and a whole lot of alcohol.

After we ordered pizza, she finally let on that she and Vic had been playing cat and mouse for the past few days and that she was thinking of giving him a real shot. The thing with Izzy is that she's a commitment-phobe. She's absolutely terrified to commit herself to someone, but apparently Vic broke through her barriers and she's giving him a chance.

Having Izzy distracted with Vic leaves me free to spend time with Trevor without having to question everything around us and constantly look over my shoulder. Of course, part of the appeal with the sneaking around is the actual thrill of sneaking around. Obviously I'm wildly attracted to Trevor—I'm not sure how any red-blooded female couldn't be—but am I still going to find our rendezvous as tempting when we can be out in public? Or even worse, what if I'm unable to keep my feelings for him and the sex separate? Because all it would take is one integral moment for me to fall head over heels in love with him. Truthfully I'm almost there already, and that scares the shit out of me because I'm leaving Dale City in a week and a half. I have to. My life and my dreams are in Hollywood.

"Hey, there you are," Izzy jokes as she brings me back from the void I'd fallen into.

I take in her nervous expression and the way she rocks back and forth on her heels. Her anxiety fills the room and my instincts sprout forth.

"Hey, Izzy, you look outstanding in that dress. Please keep it."

"Oh," she says absentmindedly as she looks down at the red jersey dress she borrowed from me. It's cinched at her waist and cascading down her thighs, ending at the knees. "Thanks. So, um, will you be okay tonight? "

"Of course. You go have fun with Vic. Actually, I think Trevor mentioned taking me somewhere tonight. So maybe I'll do that," I add nervously, but not surprisingly, Izzy misses the mention of Trevor and continues to gaze down at her dress. Standing from the bed, I walk over to my best friend and wrap her in my arms. "Hey, Iz. I can stay home with you if you want. You don't have to go on a date with him. I can see him out."

"I want to go out with him," she says as she rests her head on my shoulder. "I like him, a lot. More than I ever thought I could like someone."

"Iz, are you still…?" By the way she doesn't meet my eyes, I already have the answer. My best friend and femme fatale is still holding onto her innocence. She talked a lot of talk but never once let anyone past her barriers. "Hey, don't worry. You don't have to do anything you don't want to do. And I don't know Vic well, but he seems like the kind of guy who would be patient with you. And hell, if he's not, just tell your brother. I'm sure Trevor would love to try and kick his ass."

Finally I small smile creaks across her lips as she leans back out of my arms. "Try. Vic would crush him."

"True," I add as I notice Vic turning into the hallway. "So go, have a good time. I expect you to tell me everything tonight."

Izzy's face changes as she turns and notices Vic, so I tack on "Or tomorrow. Have fun, you two."

"Bye, Quinn," Vic states as he rests his hand on Izzy's lower back and escorts her from the house.

Just as I hear the door close, I dart for my cell phone resting on the nightstand and type out a message for Trevor.

Me: I'm ready

Trevor: Be there soon

*

THE WIND WHIPS THROUGH my hair as Trevor navigates the winding back roads toward Houston. When he arrived at the house half an hour ago, I was struck dumb by how sexy he looked in a pair of camo cargo shorts, a black T-shirt, and a black hat. So simple and casual, and so very Trevor. My knees actually grew weak when I let him through the door, and I had to hold onto the doorknob like a life vest in a sea of sexiness. When I turned back around to find him leaning against the opening to the living room, casually taking in my appearance, I actually had to wipe the drool from the corner of my mouth. His eyes were full of heat and promise, and I was drowning in them, hoping with all I have that he'd throw me a raft as I made my way over to him.

And I wasn't disappointed.

Trevor snatched me when I was standing about a foot away from him and hauled me close, meshing our bodies into one. I had hoped he was going to kiss me, my eyes begging for it as I puckered my lips slightly. Instead, his fingers left a hot trail from the back of my thighs as they meandered upward toward the rough hem of my shorts. His touch scorched me as it followed the seam connecting my ass to my legs, and I gasped when he gripped the bottom of my shorts.

"I fucking love these," he said into my ear, his gravelly tone brushing across my skin, heating me on the inside.

"Your cheeks are red. What are you thinking about over there?" Trevor asks, breaking me from my internal musings. I wished he would've taken me against the wall in the foyer—I damn well would've let him—but he had quickly ushered me to the car, adjusting his shorts along the way.

"Just daydreaming," I lie as I go back to gazing out the window.

The skyscrapers of Houston stand proud off in the distance and shimmer in the light of the setting sun. Brilliant oranges, pinks, and reds reflect and twinkle in the mirrored panels of the buildings, a kaleidoscope of colors gleaming in the evening light.

"I forgot how gorgeous it is here at night, the way the light reflects off everything," I gush.

"That's part of the reason why we're going this way. I wanted you to have something nice to remember from your visit," Trevor replies.

"I have a lot of nice things to remember from this visit," I tell him, my meaning coming through loud and clear.

And as I had hoped, he turns to look at me underneath the brim of his hat and smiles in thanks.

"I'll probably miss you when you leave. Not a lot, because you're annoying as fuck, just like my sister, but I'll miss you a little," he says in jest, obviously wanting the mood of the evening to stay lighthearted.

"Aw, you're too kind. I'll probably miss you a little too. Just enough to remember why I don't need to take extended trips to Dale City."

We both chuckle, though it's forced, as the realization of my trip ending is closing in.

A large building of concrete and glass begins to ascend into the horizon, and I perk up. "Where are we?" I ask as we pull into the parking lot.

I'm surprised when we don't stop but make our way toward the back of the building where several loading docks are filled with trucks backed into their open spaces. The car jerks as Trevor puts it in Park, and it brings my attention back to him.

"A friend of mine co-owns this brewery. I thought it would be something fun and different. And I don't need to mention that the food is some of the best I've ever had."

"Ooo, I should tell your mother that," I tease as I unbuckle my seat belt.

"Don't worry, she's well aware. We eat here pretty frequently now that Dad is getting close to retiring."

"I feel terrible that I haven't been over to see them more since I've been here, but it's so hard with them living across the street from my parents—er, the people who… damn, what the hell do I call them?" I ask in frustration as he leads me into a side door.

"They're still your parents. They raised you from birth. And my mom would love to see you more. I can ask her to stop by during the week. But you know, you're always welcome to family dinner on Friday."

"I can't believe y'all still do those."

"We do, though usually only once a month now though. But with you in town, my mom's been itching to host more."

"Well I can't wait. But please make sure it's okay with them first."

As we approach a solid steel door, Trevor knocks three times.

"Quinn, you know they've always thought of you as family."

The door opens to a heavily bearded man who smiles widely when he sees Trevor.

"Hey, man. Glad you could make it. I have everything set up."

"Thanks, Mike. I appreciate you doing this for me."

"No sweat. It's not every day we get this caliber of company" Mike glances at me and winks. "I mean, the famous Officer Shaw is dining in my establishment and drinking my beer. What more could I ask for?"

Relief floods through me as I realize Trevor set this up so I wouldn't feel out of place or like an outcast. An empty banquet room opens before us, and I home in on the single two-person table in the corner overlooking the tree-lined field to the right, copper brewing kettles and a tasting room all behind large-paned windows to the left.

"Don't worry, no one can see in here. That's the beauty of this room," Mike explains as he realizes my trepidation of people in the tasting room recognizing me.

"Thank you," Trevor says as Mike escorts us to the table and then introduces the waitstaff serving us tonight.

Trevor and I peruse the beer menu and both settle on a wheat beer, which, by the look of surprise on his face, he did not expect from me. I like surprising him.

"What? I'll just have to hit the gym hard tomorrow. Thank goodness Izzy got me a visitor pass for my time here."

Our beer arrives quickly, and we place our orders as the nervous waiter averts his gaze from me. Something I've grown accustomed to from people, unfortunately. Either they're too nervous to even speak to me or they act like they've known me their entire lives; rarely is there a happy medium. In LA I can't even run to the grocery store for a tub of ice cream without having my security detail follow along.

And now I realize the beauty of this date with Trevor. He brought me to a place where I could be myself and feel safe. Damn if he isn't Mr. Fucking Perfect.

"Hey, Trevor," I start as I take a sip of my beer and let the alcohol fuel my courage. "Thank you for taking me somewhere private and for keeping an eye on me. I know you've been checking in around town while I'm here."

He nods. "You're welcome. I know we haven't had any photographers step foot into Dale City as of yet, and I want to keep it that way. Your safety is my priority, but don't worry, it's absolutely not a hardship on my part." He winks and takes a healthy gulp of his beer as we watch a crowd of people our age stroll into the tasting room. For a Wednesday night, the brewery is packed.

"You think they're the same age as us?" I ask curiously as one of the guys smacks another guy on the shoulder in a joking manner, causing him to spill some of his beer.

"Probably."

The way they all interact makes me feel older than my twenty-four years. I never experienced this part of adulthood: the post-college fun, serial dating, careless sex. I've always been on the straight and narrow. Achieve one dream and check it off the list, then move on to another. And as an actor, I need to act and present myself as more mature than the others in the field to be taken seriously. I didn't just dream of an acting career for the money or notoriety—acting is my everything. Even if I never read another script for the rest of my life, I could see myself starting a drama course for aspiring actors. Actually, that's on my goal list as well.

Turning my attention back toward Trevor, I watch him take in the crowd on the opposite side of the glass. The serious look in his eyes has me contemplating if the cop in him is rising to the surface, or perhaps he feels the same way I do. Izzy doesn't speak much about her brother when we catch up on the phone, but I know it takes a lot of time and pride to be a cop.

"Did you get to do anything wild and crazy?" I ask, drawing his awareness back to me.

"Naw, I joined the academy shortly after graduation. I did night school for a while to appease Mom, so I do have a bachelor's degree in criminal justice."

"That's amazing, Trevor. I had no idea. I wish I had taken the chance to go to college. I planned to apply to UCLA, but then my career took off so I never had the chance. And my days are long like yours. Twelve hours, typically."

"You could still do college, Quinn. There isn't a certain age cap on it. Now that your career is steady, you could look into some online courses. What do you think you'd study?"

"I had thought about teaching," I reply nervously, taking another drink.

"Teaching?" he asks, clearly surprised, and I know he's thinking what I have for years: that I would make an awful teacher, that I wouldn't know what to do with students.

"Forget it. It's just a silly idea."

"No, no," he rushes out and places his hand on top of mine. "I think it's a great idea. You'd make an amazing teacher, Quinn. I'm guessing drama?" I nod and he continues, "Who better to show students how the industry works than a professional? I don't think it's silly at all. You should do it, absolutely."

His belief in me is astounding. I had doubted myself for so long, first with acting and then with my next steps in life. But to hear him praise me and have confidence in my skills has a new warmth blooming in my soul.

"Thank you."

"No thanks are needed, sweetheart."

The waiter stumbles back into the room as he carries the tray loaded with our food. I watch in horror as it tips sideways, but luckily Trevor jumps from his seat and grabs the edge, keeping the tray upright and our food from crashing to the floor.

"My apologies. I seem to have two left feet tonight. I'm usually not so careless," the waiter embarrassingly admits as he shoots flitting glances in my direction.

"No harm, pal."

Trevor pats the waiter's back and takes his seat as the waiter places the food before us. My mouth waters at the smell of the juicy brisket.

"This looks amazing," I exclaim as I eye all the delectable food on my plate. The presentation is almost as breathtaking as the scents in the air.

In response, Trevor admits, "Yes it does," and I find him watching me through those stunning green eyes, a sexy side smirk on his mouth.

I've had photographers, directors, and fans all give me words of flattery and I have never once believed them, thinking they all wanted something from me and my career. But with Trevor, I can feel the sincerity in his compliment, and for the first time in my life, I believe it.

"So, I'm going to come out and say it," I start as I take a hearty bite of brisket from my fork.

"Shoot."

"How can you still be single?"

"Very easily."

"No, that's not what I meant. Why? Why are you still single? You've been nothing but charming and nice to me. Not to mention you have a steady job and income, your own home, and well, frankly, you're fucking sex on two legs. So explain it to me."

The fork clatters as he sets it down on his plate, resting his elbows on the table and steepling his fingers in front of his mouth. At first I'm afraid I've stepped out of line and I willingly prepare an apology, but just as I'm about to beg for forgiveness for my intrusion, Trevor begins to speak.

"It's not that I want to be single, I just am. A couple of years ago there was someone I was serious with. I actually thought we were heading in the right direction, you know?"

Yeah, I know. And that knowledge burns like an ulcer in my stomach.

"I got hurt on the job, gunshot to my thigh during a typical stop for speeding. The guy was in a stolen car with five warrants to his name. He shot me at point-blank range. I think he was hoping to hit my goods, but his aim was off due to whatever drugs he had been doing at the time. Anyway, it burst an artery and I was rushed to the hospital with severe blood loss. She came into my room with tears streaming down her cheeks and said she couldn't do it. That she couldn't handle my job. The next day my mom said she had moved out. I haven't heard from her since."

My eyes must be bugged out of my head, because utter shock is an understatement to how I feel at this moment. Who in their right mind could walk away from someone, especially someone they care about, when they're lying in the hospital bed?

He must notice my rising alarm because he quickly adds, "In her defense, her father lost his life in the 9/11 attacks in New York City. I understood where she was coming from, and I hold no ill will toward her."

"Did you… did you love her?"

"I thought so. Now? I'm not so sure."

His words should soothe me, but they don't. Now I'm on a high emotional alert, a rollercoaster that I desperately want to get off but keep strapping myself in for the ride.

"Now it's your turn. Tell me, Quinn Miller, why is it that you're unattached and available?"

I should've expected the tables to turn. Of course, he'd want to know why I'm not seeing anyone, but that answer is a simple one.

"Because dating anyone in my world is a recipe for disaster. It's just easier being single."

Trevor doesn't believe a word of it based on the patient look he's giving me. Probably a look I should master if I ever plan on becoming a teacher, because at this moment I'm itching in my seat ready to spill my guts.

"Ugh, stop with the stare."

"Well, I know that isn't the entire story, so spill."

"I met Alex Cruz on the set of my first movie," I begin, but then Trevor practically spews the beer from his mouth as he recognizes the actor's name.

"Alex Cruz, the action hero? The star of the *Blood Brothers* franchise? The guy who's been in and out of jail for the last five years?"

"Yep, that's the one. It was all over the tabloids. I'm surprised you didn't know."

"Sorry, I don't follow entertainment things usually."

"Well when I met him, he was just starting out, like me. Anyway, he charmed me and pretty much rode my coattails as I succeeded. Then when he had name recognition in the industry, he just up and left. I wasn't sad about the breakup—I had seen it coming for a while, and so did Priscilla—but it still hurt. I had given him everything." I swallow the remainder of my beer and place the glass back on the table with a clatter.

"Everything?" Trevor inquires, but I know he understands what I meant, so I just shrug in acknowledgment.

The waiter comes in to dispose of our plates, utensils, and glasses, keeping Trevor from saying anything more; instead, he emits a low growling noise under his breath.

"Hey, it's fine. I'm fine. And now I'm here with you."

His eyes soften marginally as he tosses a few bills on the tabletop.

"Did you want to go to the tasting room?" I ask as he stands from the table and pulls my chair out for me.

"No, I have something else planned for tonight."

"Are you going to tell me what that might be?"

Escorting me from the banquet room and back down the hall, Trevor rests his hand on my back, just above the curve of my behind, squeezing gently as he shakes his head, ignoring my question.

"So mysterious, Officer Shaw."

"A little suspense never hurt anybody."

Back at the car, he helps me tuck into the passenger side before jogging around the front and sliding into the driver seat. Before doing anything else, he reaches over and tugs on my seat belt, making sure it's secure before fastening his own. Wide-eyed, I stare at him in wonder.

He simply shrugs and says, "Safety first," before starting the car and putting it in Drive.

We exit the brewery and turn in the opposite direction, and my interest begins to pique. I trust Trevor with my life, and I know whatever he has in store will be amazing, just like the date thus far.

Just like him.

RENEE HARLESS

CHAPTER SIXTEEN
Trevor

*I*T FELT GOOD TO open up to Quinn during dinner. Only Izzy and my mom know what truly happened with Beth, everyone else assuming I had broken things off between us. It wasn't too long before the playboy ways of my high school years were making themselves known again.

I didn't care for the assumed title, nor did I actually practice it. But I never squelched any of the rumors that milled about town, and there were plenty of women in Dale City who liked to say they had a wild tryst with me at some point in time.

But looking at the sweet innocence on Quinn's face as she stares out beyond the window, I almost wish I had killed each and every allegation. She's just as kind and pure as she was growing up, and she deserves someone far better than the likes of a town playboy.

Tonight though. Tonight I'm going to treat her right—how she should expect to be treated by every man from here on out. I'm going to set the benchmark so she knows that if she ever settles down, she's found someone worthy of her.

The store Mike mentioned comes into view, and I quickly run inside to grab the items that were ordered for me. Five minutes later, I jump into the car and take us back toward Dale City.

We travel in silence, the radio playing a current pop song, until the road I'm looking for comes into view. The fields we used to run through as teens look different when you're coming from the opposite direction, and I'm quite certain that Quinn has no idea where we've come.

The owners of the farm have been friends with my family for years, which is why we were never in trouble when we made our way to the clearing during the night hours. We always thought we were being so sneaky, but the only reason my parents allowed it was because they knew we were safe on the property.

Last night I called in a favor with the family to set something up for us in the clearing. Nothing big or fancy, but something to help erase the bad memories that

Quinn's formed since she's been home. Something for her to remember me by other than the incredible sex.

"Follow me, sweetheart," I request as I hold a hand out to her while the other rests on the door, holding the bag.

"Where are we? Are we going to get into trouble?"

I gasp in mock admonishment and stop dead in my tracks, practically yanking her back with me. "Are you accusing a servant of the town of Dale City of causing trouble and mayhem, Ms. Miller?"

"Um... yes?" she says more as a question and not a statement, but the smirk on her face lets me know she's playing along. I love that she gets my sense of humor.

"Well, if I'm causing trouble, then you, Ms. Miller, are an accomplice. Therefore, if we're going to cause trouble, we better do it right." A plan begins to form in my mind, and I know the perfect way to have her stumble upon what I've set up for her tonight. "You have until the count of three. One."

"Wait, Trevor, I'm not—"

"Two."

"Come on, what are you—"

"Three."

And just as expected, her competitive nature takes over and she begins rushing through the cornfield, following the path laid by years of servicing plants. I keep close, letting her think I plan to catch up and race past her, but always one step behind.

When I know we're close, I slow my pace, allowing her to take in the scene created just for her.

As I come into the clearing, I'm flabbergasted. I only requested a setup of the string lights I provided, a cooler, and a small stereo for music, but this looks like something out of a storybook. There's a gazebo in the middle of the opening with lights strung between the posts and columns, illuminating the wooden structure and the space surrounding it. Inside the gazebo rests an ice-filled bucket on a bar stand with a bottle of champagne emerging from the top. And, almost awkwardly, a blown-up air mattress sits on the edge of the clearing in a darkened space. I suppose it's a good night for stargazing, and I pray my parents and their friends had that in mind when they set this up.

"Trevor... this is... amazing. I don't even know what to say."

"You don't have to say anything. I did this to give you a good memory here, something to remind you of all the good things in Dale City."

Spinning around, she pins me with her brown eyes and a seductive smile spreads across her lips as she steps toward me, placing her hands delicately on my hips.

"Something good, like you?"

"You know, like Izzy, this clearing, growing up here… and yeah, me."

"I always think kindly of my memories with you and your sister, and now I'll have this amazing memory. Thank you." She lifts onto her toes and presses her lips against mine.

This moment could easily turn into something more. It wouldn't take much for me to sweep Quinn into my arms and haul her over to the mattress in the shadows, but I hold myself back. Instead, I rest my palms on both of her cheeks, and mimic her kiss before pulling back.

"Come on, I have something for you."

I carry the bag in one hand while the other holds tightly to Quinn's. As we step onto the wooden planks of the gazebo, I'm not surprised to find two wineglasses resting underneath the ice chest. I grab those and then snag the champagne bottle from its chilled container.

Releasing Quinn's hand, I take a seat cross-legged in the middle of the gazebo and gesture for Quinn to do the same. With a twist of my body, I flick on the stereo, which is tune to the same pop station we were listening to in the car. Not my favorite type of music, but it seems to please Quinn so I leave it there.

"I bet you know some of these singers, don't you?"

"Not personally, but I have run into them a time or two. I'm surprised you listen to this stuff. Doesn't really fit you, if you know what I mean."

"You're right, I'm definitely more rock and roll, but I can deal with it in the background. Izzy was the last passenger in my car, which should explain the station choice."

"Her silly rule that the person riding shotgun always gets control of the radio."

I admire the long column of her neck as Quinn tosses her head back in laughter. Unfortunately, I spoil the moment when I add, "Yeah, Izzy and her stupid rules," which has us both remembering Izzy's teenage plea of us to not hook up.

"So, what's in the bag?"

Thankful for Quinn's change of subject, I pull out the small box and place it between us.

"Go ahead and open it up."

As she lifts the top of the cardboard box, the heavenly aroma fills the air around us.

"Wow," she murmurs as she stares openly at the mound of cake.

"It's a molten lava cake. Mike assured me it's the best in Houston," I explain as I take out two forks from the bag. "Shall we?"

I spear my fork into the heaping mass and watch in wonder as the liquid chocolate pools out from the center. Scooping some onto my fork with the cake, I hold it out toward Quinn, offering her the first bite. She doesn't disappoint. Her plump lips open and then wrap around the morsel, her tongue peeking out to savor the remaining chocolate on her lips as I pull the fork free.

Quinn lets out a rumbling groan as she tosses her head back and closes her eyes. Her body says it all—she's in ecstasy. It takes every ounce of my self-control to keep from pouncing over this dessert and making her moan like that for hours. Alternatively, I scoop another mouthful onto my fork and hold it out for her to taste again.

"Mmm," she moans as she quickly consumes the second piece of cake. "Aren't you going to have any dessert?"

"Sweetheart, my dessert is watching you enjoy each bite."

"Well, I'm certainly not going to turn it down."

She finishes the cake after a few more bites, forcing me to eat a few as well, and sips her champagne.

"This is really beautiful. They should keep it like this all of the time."

I have to agree, and I'm certainly going to mention it to the owners tomorrow when I thank them for setting it up. But I'm distracted by the small sigh that emanates from Quinn's lips, her slight sound of resolution.

"What's up, Quinn?"

"Nothing," she replies, but I give her a skeptical glare, showing her I don't believe a single word. "Really, it's nothing."

I know she isn't being forthcoming, a trait I'm not fond of, but I leave her be. The song on the radio changes and it's one I recognize: a song about childhood friends who become lovers and more. To me, the song reminds me of a modern version of "Wonderful Tonight" by Eric Clapton.

On instinct, I stand up with my glass and then take Quinn's, placing both on the flat railing. I hold out my hand, and when she takes it, I pull her close and do something I never imagined I would get the chance to do with Quinn—we dance. It's not artistic or theatrical, just a subtle sway to the music with our clasped hands resting on my chest, her head lying against my shoulder, my arm wrapped around her waist. It's beautiful and perfect, and a memory I will never forget. Because even though Quinn will leave our lives with only promises to return, we'll always have this.

The disc jockey must know on some level what's blossoming in the gazebo because the song changes to another ballad about love, a profession of all the things I can't say to the woman in my arms. I won't hold her back or ruin her friendship with my sister; I've always cared too much about her to hurt her in that way, deprive her of the things she wants most.

Finally a commercial airs and we pull apart, the air changing around us, breaking our spell.

"Do you want to look up at the stars?" I ask. I don't miss the look of disappointment in her eyes, but being the actress she is, Quinn hides it beautifully.

"Sure, just like old times."

Yep, a time when you were only my fantasy.

The camping mattress is covered with a sheet of some sort, a quilt folded neatly at the bottom. For being out in an open field, the setup truly has a homey feel. And it's perfect for tonight.

Quinn plops onto the mattress and begins laughing as it bounces her back and forth, even more so when I join her on the inflatable. After a few minutes of situating ourselves onto the bed, Quinn tucked perfectly beneath my arms and her body curling around me, we stare up at the crystal-clear sky. From here we're far enough from the city that we don't have the residual glow of the streetlights or airport, and Dale City is small enough that they don't produce enough light to detract from the darkness of the night.

"Now that I'm here I realize how much I miss being able to see the sky like this. So open and free. Where I live in LA, you can barely make out any stars through the denseness of the fog. I have to go to the top of the building just to see the North Star. Everything else is dulled by the city lights."

Wanting to take in her expression, I twist my head in her direction. Quinn faces upward with a small smile angled on her lips. She looks… happy.

A softness brushes against my hand resting limply beside my body, and I almost startle until I recognize the dainty fingers as they link with my own. It reminds me of our last time in this very field, how I wanted so badly to make Quinn mine, but my sister was always more important to both of us. Just like she is now. But I can't bring myself to tear our fingers apart. Instead, I hold her grasp like a lifeline knowing it's one of the last moments we'll have together before she leaves on Monday.

Her pert mouth opens in a gasp and then moves silently. A shooting star must've zoomed across the sky because it seems as though Quinn is making a wish and mouthing her little chant: "I wish I may, I wish I might…."

If I could wish for anything, I know for certain it's that Izzy and Quinn's friendship stays intact. Whether Izzy finds out about our little escapades or not, I know their friendship is meaningful to both of them.

Quinn must've finally felt my stare because she turns to look me, her face only a few inches away.

"Thank you for this, Trevor. This has been one of the best nights of my life."

"You're welcome. We should probably head back soon. I know Izzy will be excited to tell you all about her date."

I start to move on the mattress, but a steady hand pins my shoulder to the bed, its strength surprising me. Her soft, supple body presses against my hardened muscles and I grow in need.

"Trevor, I want you to make love to me."

"Here?" I ask, my voice cracking like a prepubescent teenager.

"Yes, here."

My attempts to argue are futile because as she merges our lips together, something about her kiss possesses me and I lose all train of thought as to why this is a bad idea. Power inside me surges, and I flip us over so I'm resting on top of her delicate body. My hunger for her is overwhelming, and she seems equally as intoxicated with lust.

"How bad do you want me, sweetheart? You want me to take you here in the middle of the field?" I growl as I yank off my shirt and toss it onto the bed beside us.

"God, yes." Quinn arches her back for me as I reach around to remove her shirt. I need to feel her, all of her, pressed against me.

We make quick work of our clothes and dispose of them on the bed next to us. By her heavy pants, I can tell passion is surging through her veins just as it is mine.

A warm breeze travels across our naked bodies, and in the dim light of the gazebo, I watch in fascination as goose bumps pebble across her skin and her nipples harden into inviting peaks. A craving to have them in my mouth is overwhelming, so I eagerly bend down and capture the seductive tip between my lips. I alternate between licking and sucking on the sweet skin until I have Quinn writhing beneath me, rocking her sex against my cradled thigh. I move to the other side and repeat the motion, bringing Quinn to her pinnacle but never over.

"You want more, Quinn? I could savor these sweet strawberries all night."

She grips my hair, telling me without words how much she enjoys my play and how much more she wants. I let her bring my head up toward her face, where she kisses me almost sloppily, her body too revved to care about perfection. Her hips rock against my thigh, coating my leg in her heat, and I know she's seeking something to get her off.

With a tug on her bottom lip, I pull back and leave a wet path of kisses and licks from her chest down to her navel. Resting one hand on her hip, I slide the other through her womanhood, her pussy soft and wet. With a gentle flick of my tongue, I give her clit the attention it deserves, and Quinn practically jackknifes off the bed. My movements are slow and steady, wanting to take my time memorizing each and every nuance to Quinn's pussy. How every time I slide my tongue against her slit, she practically purrs in satisfaction, her muscles tightening around my finger and pulling me in farther.

I guide her closer to her orgasm until she falls over the edge, her nails digging into my shoulder as she cries out. Too lost in watching her come apart, I don't notice as her hand travels across her hips and reaches for my cock. The groan that falls from my lips is deep and rich as she strokes my shaft a few times before aligning it with her center.

"I want to feel you," she whispers as she removes her hand and leans up on her elbows to watch.

And fuck, if that isn't sexy as hell, my girl wanting to watch me slide deep inside her.

I rear back and widen her bent thighs, spreading them apart as I align my cock with her sex. I want to take it slow, need to, but my craving is too great and I fill her completely with one thrust.

Quinn cries out, a mixture of pain and pleasure at my intrusion, but I can do little to stop. Quick and hurried, I guide myself in and out of her heated center. The animal inside me takes over and I plunge myself into her, marking her body with each thrust.

It doesn't take long before the familiar tingling develops along my lower spine and my sack tightens almost painfully.

"Come on, sweetheart. I need you to come," I beckon, wanting her to find her release before I let mine take control. Reaching down, I hold onto her hips as I pull away from her body, Quinn's cry of protest weakening my resolve. With a twist, I flip her onto her stomach and tug her hips back, lifting them into the air. I stand from the mattress, planting my feet firmly on the ground and tug her hips back until she's at the perfect height for my cock.

I slide into her sex again and Quinn moans as she pushes back, meeting my lunge.

"Fuck, you feel good this way," I growl as I slap her perfect globe right at my hip. Her sex clenches as she barks out in pain.

"I'm going to come, baby. I need you to come."

"Almost there," she pants as she rocks back into me harder and I increase my speed. I slap her behind once more and her quivering muscles grip me tightly as she explodes from her orgasm.

My release follows closely behind hers, and I relish in the sight of my cum spilling from her slit as I slide free from her channel. Leaning over her relaxed body, I press a kiss between her shoulder blades as she lies weakly on the bed, her eyes closed but a smile on her face.

"That was amazing, sweetheart."

"Mmhmm," she sighs without opening her eyes.

Walking barefoot over to the gazebo, I grab the leftover napkins from our dessert and clean myself, then Quinn.

"All right, sweet girl, let's get dressed. I should probably get you home," I say as I notice the late hour on my watch.

Wrapping herself in the quilt, she rolls over and gestures for me to join her.

"Can't we just stay a little longer?"

"Yeah." I wrap her in my arms. "We can stay a little longer."

RENEE HARLESS

CHAPTER SEVENTEEN
Quinn

LURRY-EYED, I REACH OVER to silence the alarm on my phone as it wails on the nightstand. It's six in the morning, and Trevor and I stayed buried underneath the quilt out in the clearing until about midnight. Which isn't late by any means, but my body was so completely relaxed and drained that I passed out once he set me in the car.

Unfortunately, it means I missed catching up with Izzy last night, and I know she was dying to tell me about her date with Vic. Hell, *I'm* dying to hear about her date with Vic.

I take note of her footsteps outside my door and know she's heading into the kitchen for her morning cup of coffee. I quickly toss the blankets off my body and amble out of the room.

"Good morning," I call out as I snag a mug from the cabinet and pour myself a cup of coffee before taking a seat at the table. "How was your night?"

Izzy stays silent, her eyes calculating until she takes a sip of her coffee and relaxes into her chair.

"It was great. Perfect, actually."

"Oh, Iz, that's awesome. I want to hear more."

"How was your night? You came in really late." She grabs a banana from the fruit basket in the middle of the table and then bends her leg up onto the chair.

"My night was really good. Trevor and I did some script reading, and then he took me to a brewery his friend Mike owns. I'm sure you've been there. The place was amazing, and they gave us a personal tour and everything." I extend the truth, trying to cover up what we did the rest of the evening. "He took back roads I never even knew existed. The sky was beautiful."

"I like that brewery. The food is really good."

"I had the brisket and oh my goodness, it melted in my mouth."

Izzy stays quiet, sipping on her coffee and nibbling her banana as she takes me in and weighs my words.

Finally she asks, "What do you plan to do today? I have to go in early for a staff meeting."

"Oh, I'll probably just hang around and memorize the script some more. Maybe venture downtown. Actually, do you want to meet for lunch? Trevor mentioned a good Chinese restaurant that opened a year ago."

"Yeah, Chinese sounds good. Meet you at eleven thirty?" she asks as she stands from the table and disposes of her banana peel and empty mug.

"Sure, I can't wait."

I spend a few hours going over the script, trying to get a feel for the last scene, when I notice the time.

Piling into my old car, I feel a bit nostalgic. I bought the new-to-me Honda Accord with money I earned from my job at the veterinarian's office in high school, using the remainder for my first apartment in LA. It carried me to California and back, and it would pain me to part with her. Everyone assumes that because I'm a celebrity, I must spend my money wildly, but that couldn't be farther from the truth. Other than the condo I paid for, my money goes to paying my agent and publicist and the rest goes into a savings account. I'm not even sure how much is in there at this point.

The ignition starts when I crank the key, and I send a silent thank-you to the car heavens.

I smile at the driver of the tractor I pass as it travels down the road more slowly than I need. To my right stands the high school, which held such wonderful memories for me. With a sudden urge, I pull into the lot. For it being summer, I'm surprised to find cars in the front parking area, but I figure summer school may be in session so I ignore it.

Although it's probably considered trespassing, I exit my car and make my way toward the auditorium. The call of the stage is beckoning me and I need to see it, if for only one last time.

I tug on the front door but it doesn't budge, so I move toward the back of the building to find the stagehand door leading to the back storage room. Just as I suspected, with a tug and a quick twist of the knob, the door swings open for me. Remembering exactly where the light switch is located, I flick it on and bathe the room in light.

Beyond me is a sad sight. A room that used to be filled with props and stage screens now lies barren, a large open space gone to waste. As I step through the storage room leading backstage, I take a deep breath, fearing the place I loved so much has gone to ruin. But I'm surprised to find all the black stage curtains clean and hanging in their positions, and the red velvet curtain is closed, not showing a single tear.

They may not fund the drama program any longer, but at least they're taking care of the stage.

The same urge I felt on the road rises inside my gut and I push forward, walking across the wooden stage until I'm directly behind the velvet curtain.

Making a dramatic entrance, I plunge my hands into the rich material, right along the seam, and tug each end to the sides, allowing me to step through the opening.

It's not as foreign as I had imagined, but as I step downstage toward the area in front of the curtain—the apron, as we called it—I feel at home. I walk across the full length of the apron once and then a second time until I'm chanting a monologue in my head.

The monologue isn't enough. Deep inside of me, rooted underneath years of scripts and plays, comes the entrance to one of my first performances.

Inspired, I begin singing the opening song to *Beauty and the Beast*. Belle was one of my first starring roles, and despite the fact that I was—and still am—a Disney junkie, there was more to the role than just a girl stuck in her own world. It was that great adventure she was after. I easily transitioned to the role of Belle because we both wanted something more out of life.

As I begin to sing the melody, remembering each step as I prance through the pretend village, I'm transported back to that sophomore performance that opened to a full house. The newspaper even had a reporter in the audience. I had been nervous, my first starring role, but the moment the lights shined down on me, I became someone else. I *became* that character. And the only time I broke free was the moment the curtain fell for the last time.

A clap sounds in the house and I stop singing, almost tripping over my feet mid-skip. As the figure emerges from the shadows at the back of the auditorium, I'm pleased to see Ms. Percell, the principal.

"Well, Ms. Miller, this is certainly a surprise, though I'd hoped you would make an appearance at some point during your visit," she says as she steps up to the lip of the apron.

I take a seat on the edge, my feet swinging freely, and smile at her. Ms. Percell had been one of my favorite administrators, always pushing us to do our best, and she made it to nearly every sporting event and school activity. She cared for her students just like they were her children and supported them in their endeavors. Everyone at the school loved her, and I'm thrilled to see she's still the principal.

"I'm sorry about that. And I didn't mean to trespass, I just... needed to be here."

"No need to apologize. It was an absolute pleasure to hear you just now. And the things you've accomplished... your parents must be so proud of you."

I want to lie, to tell her they're ecstatic with my career, but something about Ms. Percell makes you want to tell her the truth, always.

"Actually, I wouldn't know."

"What do you mean?" she asks as she pulls herself onto the edge of the apron beside me with the grace of someone half her age.

"I found out recently that I'm adopted. I never knew, not even an inkling. But it explains why my parents were less than supportive of my path in life."

"I see. Well, I can't say why your parents wouldn't be proud of you, but we all certainly are."

"Thank you, Ms. Percell."

"You're welcome, dear. Anything else on your mind?"

"Actually, yes. Why did you all cut the arts programs? You know how much the drama class meant to me and everyone else."

"Unfortunately it was out of my hands. A public school needs public funds, and the school board decides where those funds are best to be used. I did fight, and I tried to explain how much those programs meant to the community. I believe I even used you as an example, but I was overruled. And when the plays stopped, so did the community group. Now our students don't have any programs for their artistic outlets, which is sad. Especially for an old drama club member myself."

Surprised, I turn my gaze from my knees to look at her.

"You were in drama club?"

"I sure was. It was some of the best times of my life. Why do you think I came to every showing? Not just because I wanted to support the students, which I did of course, but it gave me a moment to relive my youth. And Quinn, you were always remarkable on stage. You could draw in the audience and hold their attention through an entire play. I knew you were going to do amazing things."

"Wow."

"Now, I do need to close up the auditorium, if you don't mind?"

"Oh yes, sorry," I apologize as I hoist myself back up on the apron. Ms. Percell follows me out the back door and we lock it up before moving toward the front. "Actually, how did you know I was here?"

"Same way I knew everything when you were enrolled in school—I *see* everything. Have a lovely rest of your vacation, Ms. Miller. It was nice to see you."

"You too, Ms. Percell." I wrap my arms around her and squeeze her tightly.

Back in my car, I check the clock and see I'll make it to lunch with Izzy right on time. I don't type the name of the restaurant into my GPS, choosing to just drive downtown. How hard could it be to find a Chinese place on Main Street?

Ten minutes later, I learn it's extremely difficult. I called Izzy when I didn't see any signs, and she said they're located behind the law office. Of course, I wouldn't have seen that from the main thoroughfare.

As I open the doors, I'm assaulted by the smell of soy sauce and fried egg rolls. I walk past the hostess station when I notice Izzy sitting at a corner table looking at the window.

"Hey, sorry I'm late. Have you been here long?" I ask as I take the seat opposite her.

"Just got here myself. How did the script reading go this morning?"

"It was great. And on my way here, I stopped by the school and broke into the auditorium."

"You little rebel."

I laugh. "I know, right? Anyway, I was walking around the stage singing a song from *Beauty and the Beast.*"

"Of course."

"And in walks Ms. Percell. I thought I would be in so much trouble, trespassing and all, but she was just as awesome as I remember. Did you know she was in drama club too? I had no idea."

"Me either."

"Other than that, I drove around Main Street looking like a crazy person."

"More than you already are?"

"Yep."

A server steps up to our table and takes our order. I don't even need to glance at the menu to know I want chicken lo mein and two egg rolls.

"So, tell me all about your date last night, Izzy. I've been dying to hear it."

"It was, hands down, the absolute best date I've ever been on."

"Wow."

"He took me back to his house, where he cooked me dinner. Quinn, he cooked me dinner! No one other than Trevor has ever cooked me anything. And it was delicious. Filet mignon and lobster. I mean, he cooked food better than most five-star restaurants."

"What else?"

"We just sat around on his back deck talking. Quinn, he has this beautiful ranch on the outside of town, farmhouse and all. It was breathtaking, with acres and acres of land. It was left to him when his grandfather died, and his grandmother wants him to live in it now. He's thinking of selling it, but I think it really does suit him."

"So, all you did is talk?"

Izzy's face blushes a beautiful color I've never seen on her cheeks before.

"Iz?"

"I did it, Quinn," she whispers. "And he was so gentle and sweet, didn't push me at all. And I had wanted to. Not because I thought, 'why the hell am I still a virgin?' but because it felt so right to do it with him. Like it was supposed to be this way."

"Oh, Iz. How are you feeling?"

"A little sore, but okay. Vic's called me twice today to check in and make sure I'm okay. He already asked me to dinner again tonight."

"I am so happy for you. So incredibly happy for you."

"I've known him for a while, since he's friends with Trevor, but Quinn, I think I'm falling in love with him. Is that crazy?"

"Not in the slightest."

Not crazy at all.

RENEE HARLESS

CHAPTER EIGHTEEN
Trevor

"HEY, MAN," VIC SAYS as he strolls into the office, looking a bit too smug for someone who took my sister out on a date the night before.

"Hey, how did things go with Izzy last night?"

His pierced eyebrow rises in skepticism as he turns to look at me from over his shoulder. "Are you sure you want to know the answer to that?"

I can tell my face blanches because Vic's smug smile rises as he returns to the folders he snagged from my desk. And he's right. I absolutely do not want to know what took place between him and my sister.

So far, today has been a complete hornet's nest, from the moment I got called into work at four in the morning, giving me only three hours of sleep after dropping Quinn back at my sister's house, to the five speeding tickets from my morning patrol, and now to the mound of paperwork the chief slammed on my desk once I walked into the building. Not even the paperwork would've been too bad had two of the files not contained a drug bust and a homicide. At this point I'm worried I won't be leaving my desk for another three weeks, let alone an hour for lunch.

My stomach growls loud enough to garner Vic's attention, as well as the other trainee in the room.

"Hey, man, you want me to go grab you something?" Vic asks.

"Naw, I'm okay. I'll find something quick. I have too much work to tackle."

He sighs and goes back to filing the papers, shaking his head. "You work too damn hard. You better get a promotion after this."

"Doubtful," I sigh just as the chief strolls into the office, his oversized belly hanging over the top of his pants and his shirt barely holding together by the tiny buttons fighting to stay within their loops.

"Shaw," he bellows as he takes in my workload. "I need to see you in my office."

I jump from my chair, the wheels squeaking as it slides against the linoleum, and answer, "Yes, sir," before following him toward the back of the station.

"Have a seat," the chief commands as he takes his own behind his solid walnut desk.

"Thank you, sir."

"I want you to know that it hasn't gone unnoticed how hard you've been working. Not just the extra hours but the paperwork and shit no one likes to deal with. You do it and don't complain, and I commend you for that."

"Thank you, sir."

"That being said, you've been with the department for roughly five or so years and have proven yourself time and time again. Therefore, I'm promoting you to captain. There's a hefty pay increase, and we've also been able to hire three officers from other Houston departments, which should significantly decrease your hours worked."

"Wow, Chief Stanley, I don't know what to say. Thank you," I declare in awe. My body is practically frozen to the seat. I hadn't expected this turn of events.

"Well, son, you earned it. You have about a month before we're fully staffed again, so be sure to let me know if you need to take any vacation time. Perhaps to visit a certain celebrity who's been hanging about."

"A vacation does sound nice, sir."

"All right, now get back to work. Congratulations, Trevor. I'll let you know when the promotion ceremony will take place."

I nod and then quickly exit the office. My smile must be contagious because Vic raises his head and returns the grin, then I notice his eyes dart off to my vacant chair.

Well, my chair that was vacant and now sits occupied by a magnificent waterfall of blonde waves.

"Quinn?"

She quickly stands from the chair and turns to face me.

"Hey. I, um…," she begins nervously. "I brought you some lunch."

"You did?" I ask, eyes wide as I take in the scent of Chinese food.

"Yeah, I mean, I was having lunch with Izzy and thought this would be a nice treat. I gave Vic one of your eggrolls though. I didn't know he was working." She shifts side to side on her feet timidly.

Still in shock, all I can do is repeat myself as I stare down at the brown paper bag sitting idly on my desk. "You brought me food."

"Yes, I did."

"No one's ever brought me food," I tell her in bewilderment. "Not even my mother. Holy fuck."

"Um, do you want me to take it back?" She reaches toward the bag and I promptly snag it in midair.

"Don't you dare. Vic, I'll be back in… a while. You're coming with me," I tell Quinn as I tug her across the station toward our break room and staff training area.

The building is cramped, but past the training area is a bathroom. A bathroom with a secure lock.

I don't even turn around to see if Quinn's able to navigate around the tables and mats. When I get to the bathroom, I shove her inside, close and lock the door, and then flick on the light.

"You fucking brought me food," I say as I push her against the door, my body against hers. "I need to thank you."

"Well, you don't—" she begins, but I cut her off by fusing our mouths together.

I quickly move to her neck and then to my favorite soft spot behind her ear, nipping and sucking on the delicate skin.

"What if someone hears us?" she pants as she unfastens the buttons on my pants and tugs my shirt out of my waistband.

"Don't care," I respond as I make quick work of removing her jean shorts.

I slide my hand into her panties and groan when I meet the slickness of her heat. My girl is ready.

Lifting her by the back of her thighs, I align my exposed cock with her slit and then lower her body. The tightness is overwhelming, and I frantically thrust in and out of her body, my desire fueled by my hunger for her. It's not long before our frenzied pace is bringing us both toward our release.

"Fuck, sweetheart. I'm gonna come."

"Me too," she whispers against my lips before my tongue slides inside her mouth.

Quinn throws her head back, slamming it against the door as her orgasm takes over her body. The way her muscles tug at my cock, I find myself quickly falling behind her.

Fuck, I'm going to miss the amazing sex when she leaves.

As her shivers begin to subside, I place her back on her sandal-covered feet and slide out of her sex.

I grab her shorts from where they landed on the sink, thankful I had bathroom cleaning duty this morning so I know the place has been bleached in every crevice, and kneel before her as she steps into each opening.

"Well, that's probably the best thanks I've ever received for bringing food."

Unable to fight the impulse, I place another kiss to her lips, "You can bring me food anytime."

"Hmm," she moans into my mouth.

"I want to celebrate with you tonight."

Pulling back, she asks, "What are we celebrating?"

"I was just made captain."

I open the door at her astounded face and walk into the training room, her small feet finally moving for her to catch up. Quinn launches herself onto my back and I catch her effortlessly, her smooth legs around my waist.

"Trevor, that's amazing. Congratulations."

"Thanks," I say as I spin her around, resting my hands on her flawless ass but keeping an eye on the door in case anyone walks by.

"You should celebrate with your family."

"I will tomorrow at dinner. But tonight I want to celebrate with you, in my bed, for hours and hours and hours." I rock her against my cock, which is hardening once more.

"Well, I'll see what I can do."

Kissing me once more, she moves her legs back to the floor and I mourn the loss of her body.

"Did you still want to work on the script tonight like we'd planned?" I ask as we make our way back to the entrance.

"That sounds good. Just text me when you're home."

"I will. Thank you again, Quinn." I chuckle as a blush rises on her cheeks. "For the food."

"You're welcome, Captain," the saucy minx replies as she walks out the front door with an extra sway to her hips.

That girl is going to be the death of me. Her and the Chinese food.

*

I'VE BEEN HOME FOR an hour, anxiously waiting for Izzy to leave and Quinn to come over to my house. It's probably our last night to be alone together, since tomorrow she's joining us for dinner with my family and Saturday Izzy's planned for us and Vic to go to the clearing for old times' sake. I doubt Quinn's told her that we've already spent an evening there. Lord knows I haven't said anything; Izzy would strangle me with one of her elastic hair ties. Sunday I'm sure Izzy will want to spend time with her best friend, and Monday... well, then Quinn leaves for good, and I can almost bet on my life that she won't be returning to Dale City. There isn't anything for her here.

Finally Quinn's text comes through and I jump from my couch. I'm almost too eager to see her, to claim her again. Needing to calm myself and not seem too enthusiastic, I walk around the lower level of my house, able to complete a few rounds before I stop in front of my door.

Turning back, I look at the space. It doesn't scream bachelor pad like many of my friend's places—

probably because I have a bit more money to spend thanks to my parents and a steady job—but I wonder what Quinn saw when she first stepped in. Did she like it? Hate it? I wonder what she would think about living here with me.

That jarring thought has me shaking my head to rid myself of the idea. Quinn was never mine to keep. I need to remember her as the stubborn girl she used to be and not the exquisite woman she is today.

A knock sounds and I eagerly bound over and open the door. Unfortunately, I'm greeted by a sullen teenager holding my pizza box.

"Hey, Mr. Shaw."

"Hey, Kenny," I mutter as I pull a twenty out of my pocket and shove it in his awaiting hand.

"Thanks."

Grabbing the box from him, I'm about to turn around when I see Quinn amble across the street with a skip in her step. The poor sap in front of me practically stumbles into the siding of my house with his tongue hanging from his mouth. Can't really blame the kid though. Quinn looks like a ray of sunshine after a hurricane in her short jean skirt and a tank top. With each hop, her breasts bounce underneath her shirt, the confines of her bra barely keeping them in place. Soon my own tongue's hanging out as well.

"Hi there, boys."

"Hey, Quinn," I answer smoothly, trying to mask my reaction to her.

"Who's your friend?"

She watches Kenny, obviously used to reactions like his, as she doesn't bat an eye when he clams up and presses closer to the house like he's frightened of her.

"This is Kenny. He's a senior at DC High."

"Oh, well it's lovely to meet you, Kenny," she insists as she expands her smile.

Kenny squeaks out a "Hello."

Trying to put him at ease, Quinn offers an autograph and the kid nods like a bobblehead. I laugh as I grab a piece of paper and a pen from the table beside my door, grateful now that Izzy had the thought to place it there as a catchall.

"Here you go," Quinn says as she hands him the autograph. "It was so nice of you to bring over a pizza for us tonight."

"You're… you're welcome."

The kid falls down the steps but catches himself on the railing and sprints to his car, crushing the sheet of paper to his chest. I usher a giggling Quinn into my house and close the door behind her with my foot. Walking into the kitchen, I realize I need something more than I need this pizza.

Knowing she's followed, I place the pizza in the oven on a warming setting. "Do we have to read through the script tonight?"

"We don't have to, but I'd like to get a bit more practice in. Did you want to do something else?"

Spinning around, I pin her with my gaze and can tell the moment she realizes my intentions. I stalk toward her like a hunter pursuing its prey and wedge her against the outer wall of my kitchen. Without preamble, I slide my hand from her waist down her backside and then underneath her skirt and panties.

"You. I want you."

"Yes," she moans, and I plunge a finger deep inside her, loving the way her body clamps down on my intrusion. It doesn't take long for her wetness to pool around my finger, causing my cock to struggle against the zipper of my shorts.

"Undo my pants," I order against her mouth before I thrust my tongue back in like a drug addict addicted to her unique flavor.

She quickly unleashes the button on my shorts before tugging the zipper down. The shorts fall to my ankles and I kick them away before she repeats the process with my boxer briefs, blindly moving them past my hips while rocking herself against my hand.

"Touch my cock, baby."

Quinn follows my command effortlessly, stroking me from base to tip.

"Goddamn, that feels good, baby," I growl as I shove another finger deep inside her pussy.

Her deep-seated moan fills the room, and my hunger for her grows tenfold.

"I need you, Trevor." Her voice quakes as she cries out for me.

And I'll be damned if I'll deny her my cock.

Bunching her panties in my fist, I tug harshly ripping, them from her body. With her skirt gathered at her waist, I hoist her up and move us over toward the kitchen counter next to my stove.

Her lips are plump and red from our kisses, her chest heaves up and down as she fills her lungs with air, her pink pussy is exposed and slickened with her warm heat, and her legs are spread wide inviting me in. The entire package is an invitation I cannot turn down.

Lining my cock up with her sex, I tease her with just the purple and aching mushroom tip and then pull back out, both of us groaning at the retreat. I slide back in fully and hold myself steady as she works to accommodate my size.

Her body arches as she tries to work me deeper inside her channel, and I grip her ass tighter to pull her as close as possible.

"Shit, baby." I thrust in and out of her tight core, her body shaking with every pulse.

"Harder," she cries as she braces her delicate hands against the cool granite countertop.

She commands and I obey.

The pace of my thrusts increases as I slam into her over and over again until she's crying my name out.

"I need another," I bellow as I continue to pound into her, reaching up to hold the back of her neck.

Quinn's body reacts to my new position, her muscles clamping down even tighter than before. "Oh God."

My own release building, I urge Quinn to reach hers, sliding my hand under her tank top and bra to palm her breast.

Her moans fill the room before she shouts, "Yes!"

Watching her come apart sends my own body over the edge, where I free-fall into a puddle of bliss. My orgasm is so strong that I continue to jerk as I pull free from Quinn on weak knees. Her body is lax on the counter, and she can barely hold herself up.

Somehow I garner the strength to ease her into my arms and carry her back to the living room to place her on the couch, then rush back to the kitchen—well, more like hobble—and tug my shorts back on. I grab some tissues from the bathroom, and as I walk back into the living room, I'm not surprised to see Quinn resting with her eyes closed. I gently clean myself from her legs and tug her skirt back down to cover her lady bits.

"I think you killed me," she murmurs.

"Naw, you're still kicking. But what a way to go, right? Death by orgasm."

She giggles and then groans, and my eyes rake over her in concern.

"Don't make me laugh. My muscles are weak."

"Oh, sorry. Do you want that pizza now?"

"Mmm, pizza."

"I'll take that as a yes."

"As you should."

Back in the kitchen, I pull the box from the oven, turn off the warmer, and plate us each a couple of pieces.

"So," I begin as I hand her the plate of greasy goodness, "what are we reading today?"

"Well, it's the scene I've been putting off for a while."

"And that would be?"

"The breakup scene. They're always my least favorite."

"Well, we knew it was going to happen eventually."

"Yeah," she sighs as she shovels a slice of pizza in her mouth.

That pit of bliss I'd just found myself in quickly turns into misery as I realize that our own breakup is on the horizon.

CHAPTER NINETEEN
Quinn

ZZY PARKS THE CAR in front of her parents' house, and I can finally release the breath I'd been holding. My nerves were on high alert as we pulled into the neighborhood—the same neighborhood where just a week ago, my world had been changed. My eyes were flitting across the street as we turned in, heavy with anticipation and anxiety, but luckily all of the lights in the house I grew up in were out cold.

Noticing my unease, Izzy asks if I want to sit in the car a moment before we head inside.

"Yeah, if you don't mind," I reply as I tuck a stray piece of hair behind my ear.

This is the first time I've come by since I found out I was adopted, and I'm surprised at how much it's affecting me.

"Take all of the time you need."

She pulls out her cell phone and sends a couple texts, probably to Vic and Trevor, and then she logs into a social media site. Which reminds me of a rule that Izzy and Trevor's mother always had in her house.

"Does your mom still enforce the 'no phones during family time' rule? I don't remember from last time I ate here."

Laughter explodes from Izzy as she places her phone back into her bag.

"Yes, she does, but only to an extent. We just have to silence our phones now. If it goes off during a dinner, she gets to confiscate it until we leave. The only one who's allowed a phone is Trevor when he's on call."

"Well, I'm glad to see they'll make exceptions." I laugh as I reach into my bag and silence my phone. "Are you nervous about tonight? I mean, I guess Vic's met them before, but not as your boyfriend."

"I'm silently freaking out about it, but they like him as Trevor's friend, so I'm sure it'll be fine. He's just never been to the house. We've always met at Trevor's."

"Are you worried about the money?"

"No... maybe? It's not like he doesn't know we have money. With the way people talk in Dale City, how could he not? But he may not have fully grasped it yet, and I'm afraid it may scare him off," she admits as we both gaze up at the three-story oversized colonial in front of us.

"I'm sure it'll be fine, Iz."

"I sure hope so."

I can hear her heart breaking in her chest at the possibility of Vic not being able to handle the wealth of her family, but I'm not worried about her. Vic's never struck me as one of those people. Heck, he didn't even blink an eye when he was introduced to me—he only had eyes for Izzy.

Finally we're both able to move from the car and are greeted at the door by the housekeeper, Frank. He had taken a rare night off last time I was in the house, and it's been ages since I've seen him.

"Well I'll be. Ms. Miller, how lovely it is to see you. What a beauty you've grown into," the older man praises as he lets us inside. Frank's been with the Shaw family since Trevor and Izzy were born. Their mother needed help around the house and then just kept him on as their kids grew older. He's always treated me kindly, just like the rest of the family, and he was more like a grandfather to me than my own.

"Frank, I'm so happy to see you," I say as I wrap my arms around the thin man. "It's been far too long."

"Is she here?" Izzy's mom calls from the hallway.

Sue comes around the corner and practically bounds over to me in her standard three-inch stilettos, yanking me into her arms.

"Sweet Quinn, how I've missed you," she whispers into my ear, ignoring her daughter who stands against the wall silently laughing. Holding me at arm's length, her gaze travels up and down, taking in my green wrap dress and brown wedge sandals. Her smile widens. "My, look how beautiful you are."

"Thank you, Sue." I have to keep myself from laughing at her expense since she saw me just two weeks ago, but then I remember she would video call me quite frequently with Izzy, and we haven't chatted since I've been back.

"Now the boys should be here shortly, so let's head out to the sunroom. Jake has decided to have dinner there since the night is so wonderful. I also remember that it's a special spot for you, Quinn, and as one of your last nights here, I would love to honor you."

"That's sweet of you, Sue, but you didn't need to go through any trouble for me."

I hear Frank scoff mockingly as Sue takes my arm and guides me toward the back of the house, shaking her head the entire time.

In the sunroom, Izzy and I take our seats as Frank pours us each a glass of white wine. We marvel at the beautiful sunset as it conceals itself beyond the horizon.

Heavy footsteps sound in the hall before Vic walks into the room just ahead of Trevor. The tatted-up and muscled man walks right over to Izzy and kisses her plum on the mouth in front of her mother, who blushes slightly but smiles widely.

I peek at Trevor as he greets Sue, trying not to draw attention to myself, but he catches my eye and winks. Man, just that slight recognition sends my body into overdrive, and my core clenches.

As Jake strolls into the room, assisting Frank with the platter of food, we all take a seat. The eight-person table easily becomes a game of musical chairs as Jake takes the seat at the head, Sue sits on one of his sides, and Izzy takes the other. Politely I move over a seat to allow Vic to sit next to Izzy, which leaves just the opposite end of the table and the other side available. Trevor looks over at me for a second and smirks, and I think he's going to make things weird by sitting directly beside me at the other end of the table, leaving his mom all alone, but he surprises me when he takes the open seat beside Sue and kisses her on the head before sitting down.

My heart almost bursts from my chest at the interaction, and I have to take a sip of wine to hide the huge grin growing on my cheeks.

"Well now, Quinn, you're sitting there all by your lonesome. Move over beside Trevor," the patriarch commands, and I dutifully pick up my glass and take the vacant seat on the opposite side, wondering why I'm being moved. In either seat, I'm staring at an open one. Until Jake slides his chair over a tad, stands along with Sue, and then moves her chair to the edge with his. Trevor shifts his and my seat closer to the end until I'm sitting directly across from Vic. Izzy casually rolls her eyes, not at all surprised by her parents' antics.

"There we are, now I can look at my whole family," Jake explains just as Frank begins to uncover the platters at the table.

"Dad, you know if you got a round table, you could see everyone all of the time."

"Yes, Isabel, you're right. Perhaps you and your mother can pick one out this week. Now, everyone, dig in."

The aromas of the strawberry salad and garlic shrimp pasta fill the room, and I nearly groan as I inhale deeply.

"This all looks amazing, Mr. Shaw. Thank you for having me," Vic says, and I repeat the thanks.

As my turn arrives, I'm surprised when Trevor slides the plate he filled over to me and grabs my empty one instead.

"Thank you," I murmur as he places heaping portions onto his new plate.

We eat our salads in silence until a fork rings against the china beside me.

"Well, since I have everyone here, I have an announcement to make," Trevor begins. I cautiously glance up to Izzy, alarmed to find her face blanched and her eyes bouncing between me and Trevor.

"What is it, son?"

Trevor takes an exaggerated deep breath and then looks squarely at each person before landing on me and winking.

"I received a promotion at work. I am officially Captain Shaw of the Dale City Police Department."

"Oh, Trevor, what wonderful news. Congratulations! After dinner, we'll celebrate."

"He really deserves it," Vic chimes in. "And on top of that, we were able to hire some new officers, so he won't have to pull any more odd hours in another month or so."

I offer my congratulations as well, and Trevor turns in his seat to thank me. That's when I notice Izzy sitting quietly in her chair, mumbling under her breath.

"Iz," Vic probes beside her, and as if broken from a trance, she perks up in her seat and apologizes before presenting her best wishes.

As the conversation continues around me about Trevor's new role, I'm struck by Izzy's fear over what Trevor was going to announce. Not only did her expression chill my veins, but it hurt to think she would believe I wouldn't discuss anything with her first.

Of course, I am the big liar in this entire game Trevor and I are playing, and no matter what happens, I'm hurting Izzy. Some friend I am.

My melancholy grows as we finish dinner, and by the time dessert and champagne are served, a migraine is building behind my eyes.

"Quinn, are you feeling all right, dear?" Sue asks with concern.

I perk up in my seat, feeling guilty at drifting off during the celebration.

"Yes, sorry. I just feel a headache coming, that's all."

Everyone turns to look at me, and I shrink under the scrutiny.

"Would you like to lie down? Or I'm sure Izzy could take you back to her house." Sue suggests.

I look over to Izzy, who glances at Vic quickly and then nods in agreement. Except I know she has plans with Vic tonight, and I was supposed to drive her car back to her house. And for everything terrible I've done as a friend in the past three weeks, I will not disappoint her by taking her from Vic.

"No, I'm sure I'll be fine. Please, let's continue celebrating Trevor's accomplishment."

Everyone stands from their seats, flutes refilled and steady in their grasps, and makes their way to the living room. Everyone except Trevor, who tugs on my hand as I walk past.

"Are you sure you're feeling okay?"

"Yeah, it's just a little migraine. Nothing I haven't dealt with before."

"You know I'm going to take you home and have Dad or Frank drive Izzy's car, right?" When I don't respond, he squeezes my hand. "Quinn?"

"Yeah, I figured as much. But please don't. I'll be fine."

Famous last words.

Twenty minutes later, I'm sitting on the couch trying my best to mask the agony within my head that's causing bile to rise from my stomach. Sue sits beside me on the smaller couch, chatting with Trevor on the chair next to her. Vic and Izzy are on the opposite side of the room with Jake, discussing the promising year of the Houston Astros. I simply stare off into space, focusing on a blank spot on the cream-colored wall, giving myself something else to direct my attention.

"So you'll be good to bring my car back? Quinn?" Izzy asks until I finally snap out of my fog and nod too earnestly, upsetting my migraine further.

"Yes, it's fine. You both have fun tonight."

Once the front door shuts, I rest against the couch and close my eyes, but my solitude doesn't last long. I feel a shadow fall over me and crack open an eye to find

Trevor standing in front of me, his arms crossed against his chest.

"You're paler than normal," he proclaims as his father strolls in with a set of car keys, Frank following him into the room.

Izzy's mother pats my hand motherly and adds, "You feel better, Quinn. And remember not to be a stranger."

But I barely hear her words. I'm locked in a battle with Trevor, who looks like he's gearing for war by the expression on his face.

"It's wonderful to see you, Sue, as always. Thank you for dinner." I wobble as I stand from the couch, Trevor reaching out to steady me.

"Come on, let's get you home."

"Good night," I say once more to Sue and then allow Trevor to guide me blindly to his vehicle, my eyes clamped tightly to shut out the light.

"You shouldn't have let it get this bad. Do you get migraines often?"

I don't answer until he situates me in the passenger seat and I hear him enter the driver side.

"This is only the third one I've had," I whisper. "They aren't a common occurrence."

I feel a softness press against my face as the subtle light behind my lids grows dark.

"Here, this should help. Mom always said darkness tends to keep them from getting worse. What do you think caused it?" he asks gently as the car begins to move in reverse.

I'm afraid to tell him that it came on due to the spark of anxiety at seeing Izzy's reaction to Trevor's announcement.

"I'm not sure. It was probably the wine."

"Liar. I saw the way Izzy reacted when she thought I had something else to say, and I saw the way you shrank into yourself the remainder of dinner."

With the pounding in my head, I don't acknowledge his correctness; instead, I grunt and adjust the shirt that rests on my face, deeply inhaling Trevor's masculine scent from the material.

"Quinn, there's nothing to worry about."

The jerking of the car as it settles into Park wakes me and causes the T-shirt to fall from my face. I realize Trevor has parked in front of his house, but he exits the car before I have a chance to ask him why.

He opens my door, silently unhooks my seat belt, and then plants his arms underneath my body. As he launches me into his chest, the pain from my migraine quadruples and I bury my head in his shoulder.

"Sorry, sweetheart. I'll have you inside soon. Do you want me to draw you a bath?" he asks as he carries me across the street.

Oh, what the neighbors must think.

"No bath. Just some sleep, please."

Trevor wordlessly carries me into the house and takes me into the guest room without turning on any lights, using the twilight through the window to guide him.

"Here you go," he whispers as he gently places me down. Trevor begins removing my shoes and then slowly unwraps my dress as if it contains the most precious gift in the world. His stare is unyielding as he takes in my almost bare form with care.

Draping the sheet and duvet over my body he strokes his hand across my hair as I settle. "I'll be right back, okay?"

He doesn't wait for a response, simply walks quickly from the room. I hear clicking and clanging, causing my body to jerk with each noise. Trevor reenters the room with one clenched fist and another holding a glass filled with water.

"I brought you some medicine. Can you sit up just a tad for me?" he requests as he sits on the edge of the bed beside me. I'm able to prop myself up with my elbow and open my mouth. Without a care, he places the two white tablets on my tongue and brings the glass to my lips. Tilting my head back, he follows the movement with the glass and even rests his hand under my chin to catch any stray droplets.

"There you go. Now lie back and get some rest. You'll feel better in the morning."

"Hey, Trevor," I say with tightly sealed eyes. "Thank you for taking care of me, again."

"You're welcome, sweetheart."

He brushes a kiss to my forehead, and a longing passes over me that's so overwhelming I almost gasp.

"Trevor, would you lie with me, please?"

I hear a rustling and then the bed dips beside me as he rests on top of the duvet.

"I don't want you to get any ideas. I'm in a delicate state and all," he jokes, trying to ease the sullenness in the room.

"The only thing delicate in this room is your huge ego," I murmur into his large chest as I snuggle closer to him. I listen to him chuckle, the light shake of his chest irritating my head but also rocking me gently to sleep.

"You've got to be kidding me," an irritated whisper sounds from the bedroom door after I had finally found myself in a wonderful dream, Trevor and me on a beach, relaxing in the warm Carribean water naked. "Trevor, man, what are you doing?"

The bed bounces as Trevor jumps from his spot. "It's not what it looks like."

I creak open my eyes a bit and see Vic shaking his head.

"Man, your sister is upstairs getting ready for bed and asked me to come check on Quinn. And what do I find? I find you in bed with her. I should've known at the station the other day, the way you were giddy as fuck all afternoon."

"Vic, you can't say anything. It would fucking kill Izzy."

Vic peeks over Trevor's shoulder and looks at me, hopefully noticing that the top cover is pressed against the bed in Trevor's form. He sighs heavily and shakes his head.

"You're asking me to keep this from her, and if this blows up in my face, I'm going to kill you, man. I'll keep your secret, but I will not cover for you. Get your ass back home. I'll make sure your sister doesn't come down."

I feel terrible as Vic turns and walks away, his shoulders hunched and filled with the weight of the lie Trevor and I have brewing out of control.

We should've never stayed at each other's house.

We should've tried harder to keep things hidden.

We should've never started this.

But as Trevor turns around with a spark of hope still in his eyes, I know that no matter how many times I tell myself differently, I wouldn't have changed any of my time with him.

CHAPTER TWENTY
Trevor

M
Y GUN SITS HEAVY at my waist as I strap my badge onto my chest. The sun hasn't risen yet, but the horizon has started to lighten into stunning shades of pink and light blue.

Tonight Izzy, Vic, Quinn, and I are supposed to head to the clearing as a last hoorah for Quinn before she returns to LA, most likely for good. Izzy is in denial about it but I'm not. There isn't anything to keep Quinn here. And even if I felt that I should tell her how I've been feeling, that I think I'm falling for her, it wouldn't make a difference. We agreed no feelings were going to be involved, that we wouldn't complicate things. Her

friendship with my sister is far too important to her and
to me. I'd give my sister the world if she asked.

Unfortunately, last night was probably my last
night to spend with Quinn, and she had to get that nasty
migraine. Not that I blame her, just bad timing. I had
hoped to ask Vic to take my sister out tonight so I could
have some alone time with Quinn, but I have a sneaking
suspicion that requests such as that would be met with a
dark glare and some cracked knuckles.

Jogging down my steps, I barely miss the faint
knock on my front door as I turn the corner.

To say I'm shocked and surprised to find Quinn
on the other side is an understatement. Without a
thought, I pull her into the house and press her against
the closing door, praying the migraine has disappeared.

Cradling her face in my hands, I search her eyes to
make sure she's okay and then ask, "What are you doing
here?"

"I… I don't know. To thank you, and… well I
missed you. I'm sorry I ruined our last night together."

Unable to hold back, I kiss her lips once, twice, a
third time, and then pull back just enough that my lips
brush against hers. "You didn't ruin anything. But I'm
fucking thrilled to see you right now."

Quinn leans forward and nips at my bottom lip,
unleashing the beast inside me. I press her even more
firmly against the door with my hips and consume her

mouth. Her tongue curls against mine with every pass, our hunger barely sated by the kiss.

An alarm sounds from my pocket, but I scarcely notice until Quinn jerks back against the door, panting.

"Shit, I have to go," I murmur. "I'm already late."

"I'm sorry."

"No need to apologize," I counter as I kiss her again. "Will I see you tonight?"

"You can count on it." She smiles as she turns the knob and sneaks out through.

I watch her cross the street, the blackness of the early morning covering her escape. Even after she successfully finds her way back into the house, I stare into the darkness wondering what I'll do once she's gone from my life in two days.

*

AT MY DESK, I spend my Saturday going over the paperwork for the new officers and filing all of the documentation for ongoing cases from this past week. I cannot wait until we have enough staff to deal with this, because it's my least favorite part of the job.

My phone chimes in my pocket, but I ignore it as another officer strolls into the station ready to cover the afternoon shift. As I greet him, my work phone rings and I notice Vic's number on the screen, Realizing he must've been the one to call a moment ago, I answer.

"Hey, Vic, what's up?"

"I'm just hanging with my grandmother and she was asking about you... and Quinn."

"Oh, anything in particular?" I ask as I shut down my computer.

"She wants to know if she can get Quinn's autograph."

"Oh, that should be—"

"And an invite to the wedding."

"Er... you'll have to explain that one to her."

"Don't worry, I tried. She's convinced that you'll end up at the altar one day. With each other."

I remain quiet, imagining Quinn walking down the aisle toward me, but I shake my head to remove that thought.

"Trevor?"

"Sorry, just packing up. And hey, I'm sorry about last night. Nothing happened but me lying with her until she fell asleep, and then, well, I fell asleep."

"I know, but that doesn't mean it didn't happen before."

"I'm not going to elaborate on that. Are you still coming tonight?"

"Ha, like Izzy would let me miss it. I'll see you then."

"See ya."

*

THE WALK THROUGH THE field that night seems different than my time here before with Quinn. Not only because she and I made love in the clearing a few nights prior, which was awkward as hell when I returned the washed sheets and quilt to the owners the next evening, but because this is the first time the three of us—Izzy, Quinn, and me—have stepped foot in this space together.

Maybe that's what brought Quinn and me together in the first place. Our love for Izzy is always the weld that bonded us. She's always the beacon of light in our life. Heck, if it weren't for Izzy, Quinn would've never stepped her pink-painted toes back in Dale City.

I'm the first one to arrive, and it seems so strange to find it barren once again, so desolate.

I remove my bag from my back and take out a blanket, the same one Quinn, Izzy, and I had lain upon staring at the stars so many years ago. Beneath that is a flask of whiskey and a bottle of Boone's Farm, per request of Izzy.

Just as I flick on one of my camping lanterns, setting it to a low ambient light, I notice the beam from a flashlight glowing from the path in the field. Izzy appears first, quickly followed by Vic, and then Quinn on their heels.

I greet them all and help Vic unpack his bag stuffed with another blanket and a second bottle of Boone's Farm. Izzy uncaps the bottle quickly and takes a swig. Quinn's standing off to the side, looking up at the sky. I dive into my bag and remove the clear bottle with the red liquid before I walk over to her.

"Here, this is for you," I offer.

She turns her attention to me and smiles, then reaches for the bottle, quickly uncapping it. "Thanks." She takes a sip and then another before holding the bottle down at her hips. "I forgot how sweet this stuff tastes."

"I'm sure it's been a while, now that you can get your hands on the really expensive stuff."

A beat passes as she lets my words linger in the air, a conversation between Izzy and Vic going on in the distance. "It seems so different here tonight. It doesn't have that same magic it did then, you know?"

I'm not sure if she's referring to when we were here in school, that mystery of sneaking out always amplifying that adrenaline rush, or the night we spent here not too long ago.

"Yeah, I know. Quinn, I—"

"Hey, guys," Izzy shouts from across the way. "Come sit down with us."

Quinn smiles knowing I had planned to say more, and maybe even knowing what I had wanted to say. She wraps her hand around my forearm, lugging me behind her toward the blankets.

Izzy bounces in her spot. "Isn't this nice? I've dreamed of doing this for years, ya know? Getting us all back together. And now Vic can be a part of it too."

"It is really nice," Quinn agrees. "Thank you for setting this up, Izzy. Not just tonight but the entire month. I needed this."

I almost jump when I feel something roll across my hand, but the warmth of Quinn's touch finally settles and I turn my hand upward toward her, allowing our fingers to lace just as they did so many years ago. Luckily Izzy's on Quinn's other side so she's oblivious to the gesture.

The girls begin chatting about high school and silly things we used to talk about during the nights like this, when the sky was blacker than anything we'd ever seen and the stars blinked like tiny flares leading us onward.

Izzy's phone goes off first, and she apologizes before standing from the blanket. Then mine quickly follows with messages from local friends offering me congratulations.

Congratulations?

"What's going on?" Quinn asks at the same time Izzy shouts, "How could you?"

As the blood drains from my face, I know with every fiber of my being that Quinn and I have been discovered.

Quinn stands and tries to calm Izzy down, but she wants none of it. Instead, my sister walks toward me, and just as I start to stand, she slaps me across the face.

And fuck, if that doesn't sting.

"How could you do this to me? That's my best friend!"

I can tell Izzy's working herself up, so I grasp her arm and drag her away from the blankets.

Quinn rushes beside us, reaching out to Izzy. "Please, let me explain. It's not what you think."

"You swore to me, Quinn! You promised me when we were sixteen!"

"I know. It's just—" Quinn begins, but then Izzy turns on me.

"Why, Trevor? Why did it have to be her?"

"Izzy, look—"

"No, *you* look!" She shoves her phone at me.

At first I see the pictures of me and Quinn holding hands walking down the sidewalk. Innocent enough, and then it's the captured photos of a kiss taken from a video that follows. A video of me walking with my arm slung over Quinn's shoulder and her arm around my waist. I know it's not that part that sets Izzy off though. It's the kiss as we walked away, thinking we were hidden from view as we skirted around a bush, that has my sister riled up. A moment I barely remember compared to the others but may very well be my undoing.

"Iz...."

"Don't 'Iz' me. Tell me why."

"Because she's here," I shout, instantly regretting my words knowing Quinn is listening, but pressing on regardless. "Don't look too much into it, Iz. She leaves tomorrow. Don't let this come between your friendship."

"What friendship? This is... this is... betrayal!"

"Izzy...."

"So, it was just sex to you? That's all it was?" Izzy asks in an eerie calm, one that frightens me.

"Yes. You mean too much to her for it to be anything more. We had an itch and scratched it. There was nothing else involved."

"I hate you, Trevor. You've ruined everything now!"

"Look, just calm down and we can work this out."

"Guys," Vic states as he approaches, hands in the air.

"What?" we both shout as we continue to stare daggers at each other.

"Um, I'm not sure how to say this, but Quinn left."

CHAPTER TWENTY-ONE
Trevor

Y HEART DROPS AND I ask him to explain, but all he can do is shake his head. "She started pacing when you and Izzy walked away, and when you questioned the friendship and said it was just sex, I turned to look at you all for a moment. When I turned back, she was gone. I'm sorry, man."

"Shit, I need to go find her," I say as I pick up the blanket and barely touched Boone's Farm and frantically shove it back in my bag.

"Hey," Vic says as he crouches beside me, "go find her. I've got this."

At his insistence, I stand and run my fingers through my hair as I look over to my sister, whose expression flips back and forth between worry and anger—her own Dr. Jekyll and Mr. Hyde.

My own anger is getting the best of me now. I can barely see past the red glazing over my eyes.

Spinning on my heels, I turn to run at full speed through the breakage in the field, hoping with all I have that I'm able to catch up to her. Because when Quinn leaves Dale City, she needs to know that she was never just sex to me. She was always so much more.

I make it to my parents' house where we parked our cars and see only mine and Vic's along the road, though I'm not sure if Quinn rode with them or drove herself. Taking a chance, I knock on the front door of the house, and thankfully Frank answers quickly.

"Is Quinn here? Has she come by?" I ask, wheezing as I catch my breath. I try to peer over his shoulder but am only met with the darkness of the hall.

"No, I haven't seen Ms. Miller. Is something the matter?"

My faith plummets and I snake my hands through my hair once more, tugging at the ends.

"Just… if you see her, don't let her leave, okay?"

"Yes, sir."

I jump off the porch, skipping the three steps leading to the walkway, and hop into my car just as Vic and Izzy scramble from the field. The car slides into Drive and I turn on my headlights as I approach them slowly.

"She's not here. Did she drive herself?" I ask Izzy.

"She did."

"Fuck!" I pound my hands against the steering wheel.

Vic leans into the window, resting his elbows on the opening.

"Look, I'm going to take Izzy back to the house. That way if Quinn shows up there, someone will be home. Then I'll help you look for her, all right?"

"Yeah, okay. She drives a gray Honda Accord, a '98 I believe, with California plates. Just… call me if you find her."

Vic and Izzy move to his car, and I take one last look back at the neighborhood before peeling off to head across town.

Twenty minutes later, Vic calls. "No sign of her, Trevor."

Dammit, where could she have gone?

"I haven't seen her either. I even checked the school. Let's head back to Izzy's and figure something else out."

When I arrive back at the house, the detective in me comes out in full force and I immediately go on high alert. Every nerve ending in my body is firing at will, and

I know without a single doubt that Quinn's been here, and recently.

I'm huffing as I make my way up to the front of the house, barely recalling if I've turned off my car as I open the front door with a jerk, causing it to slam into the adjoining wall.

"Where is she?" I yell at Izzy as she sits nervously on the couch, her foot bouncing up and down. A dead giveaway for any detective. A death warrant when it's your own twin.

"Trevor, maybe you should—"

"Don't you dare fucking tell me to calm down. You don't get to tell me to do anything! You're the whole reason this shit is happening in the first place."

"No," she counters as she rises from her seat and stalks toward me, venom spewing from her eyes. "You couldn't keep your dick in your pants, that's why this shit is happening."

"Really? Have you thought that maybe your best friend is the one who approached me?" I lie.

Izzy's eyes narrow as if that concept isn't anything she's entertained or believes.

"Quinn's not like that."

And she's not, but she readily agreed to our terms without a second thought.

"Where is she, Izzy?"

Hands planted on her hips, Izzy shakes her head as she hands me a folded-up note.

"She's gone."

"What!" I shout just as Vic enters the house. "She was here and you just let her fucking go?"

"Yes, I did. She walked in, grabbed her things, apologized to me and made me promise not to call you. She'll be filming out of the country for the next couple of weeks, so she'll be hard to get in touch with."

"Well this is just fucking great," I seethe as I squeeze the note in my hand, the hard edges of the paper digging into my palm, the pain almost soothing me.

"What did you expect, Trevor? She was leaving Monday anyway. Where are you going?" she asks as I move toward the guest room, needing to see with my own eyes that she's gone. "I told you guys so long ago that this would happen, and now our friendship is broken."

"Oh yes, you and your goddamn rule. Well congratulations, Izzy, you threw down a gauntlet when we were sixteen and you've won. But you forgot one thing." I brush past her as I move to leave the house, not wanting to be in my sister's presence for one second longer.

"Yeah, what's that?" she questions behind me as Vic stands in the room, torn between protecting his girlfriend and standing up for his friend. Poor guy just walked himself right into a shit storm.

"Your stupid rule just tore everything apart because I'm in love with her, Iz. I love her with everything I am, and I never got to tell her. And now she's gone."

The door slams behind me but I feel no remorse. The ache in my chest is too great to care about a dent in the wall or a shattered picture frame that may have fallen to the floor. My sister just denied me the chance to make things right with Quinn. Even if she still left, I could've taken the chance to explain things. I'm not sure why I said it was just about sex to Izzy when she asked. Maybe I hadn't fully come to terms with my feelings. Maybe I was trying to save face after being put on the spot. I'm not sure. But knowing I've hurt Quinn is the worst part of all. She deserves nothing but happiness, and I had to go and fall in love with her and let my pride control me.

"Hey, Trevor," Vic calls out from the porch as I head down the walkway. "You should try the airport."

I turn around and look at him in surprise. He nods and I realize Izzy told him where Quinn's headed.

I hop into my car and consider chasing after her or calling in a favor to the Houston department to track down her car and pull her over. It would give me enough time to make things right.

But I can't do that to her. I should let her go. I should let her move on. She should to be with someone better, someone who can love her and give her everything she needs. Because she isn't going to find what she dreams of with a cop in a small town who reminds her of everything she ran away from. I don't want her to live her life regretting everything, regretting me. But my desire to have her is too strong and I can't hold back my urge to rush after her, to find a way to keep her.

CHAPTER TWENTY-TWO
Quinn

M Y CAR ONLY MAKES it to the Houston airport. Not because it can't physically keep going, but my brain has turned to mush and my heart is just a pile of ash in my chest. It's dark out and I find a place to park the car, taking note of the mechanic's name on the billboard across the street. I jot down the number and hope he's able to use the car or sell it for parts.

I snag my bag from the seat and reach into the glove box to remove anything I'll need before I close the door and step away. In the jumbled mess, I find a clear rectangle dangling from a keyring with a picture inside of Izzy, Trevor, and me at an amusement park the summer before our sophomore year. Izzy and I were squeezing each other tightly, looking at the camera with silly grins on our faces. Trevor stands on my other side, holding a pair of bunny ears onto Izzy's head with his arm fully extended. I must not have thought much about it as a teen, but as I look closer at Trevor's face, I notice that he wasn't looking over to Izzy like I had always believed. He was looking down at me with the small smirk I love so dearly.

I stare at the reminder, wanting so desperately to go back to the time when we could be together like this without complications. Trevor repeated over and over again that we were to keep feelings from getting involved, but it didn't matter. I've been in love with him since I was thirteen, and I was far too naïve when we started out three weeks ago to believe that those feelings would change. I thought they were gone, but they were simply buried deep within me, waiting for their chance to blossom.

Three weeks. That's all the time I spent with Trevor, and yet it's like I've been reawakened. I do feel bad for what transpired with Izzy, but as I grabbed my clothes and hightailed it from the house, I told her that she needed to choose her brother. I wasn't going to come between them. They mean far too much to me for that. She hadn't argued with me, but even if she had it was a moot point. I wasn't changing my mind.

The note I left him had been short and to the point, nothing more than a few sentences of me wishing him the best and that I hope he and his sister would remain as close as they used to be. That I never regretted my time with him but that I do regret it ruining my friendship with Izzy. If he looks close enough, he'll find my tears blotting some of the ink and paper.

The first thing I do when I walk into the airport is stare at her and Trevor's number, my finger hovering over the Delete button with their contact information. I don't want to be tempted to reach out to them. But I can't bring myself to follow through; even in all of this turmoil, they're still my life.

I also learn why my publicist didn't give me a heads-up about the pictures: my phone's still on silent from my dinner with the Shaws the night before. I have twelve missed calls from my agent and five from my publicist. I send them both messages asking for a few days to settle back into the Hollywood scene before we address the tabloids. I just hope this doesn't bring problems to Trevor's doorstep.

The keychain stays tight within my grasp as I navigate the terminals, only relieving it when I go through security. I pull the ball cap down over my eyes as I make my way toward my gate when I notice eyes following my every move.

Finding a seat in the corner, I hunch forward and let the keychain swing from my finger, watching as the light from the ceiling catches on the plastic every once in a while. For the late hour, I'm surprised to see so many people coming and going in the airport, but then again, I don't travel this way very much so I wouldn't know.

I lose track of time as I sit hypnotized by my tiny trinket until suddenly I hear my name shouted across the terminal. And not just any shout, a cry of pure desperation.

"Quinn!" I hear closer to me, and I look up to find a frantic Trevor shoving his hands through his hair.

"Trevor?" I stand from my seat and he rushes toward me, jumping over a few chairs and frightening airline passengers as they wait for their flights.

"What are you doing here?" I question as he pulls me in tight, tucking my head against his chest. I breathe him in as I listen to his heartbeat pound beneath my ear. "How did you get past security?"

Pulling back, I look into his watery eyes as he holds up his badge in his left hand.

"The TSA have been very accommodating, especially when asked if they saw a celebrity rush through." He takes a deep breath and runs his hands over my hair, then shoulders, and finally my arms. "Why are you leaving, Quinn? Why are you running away?"

"Trevor, I can't come between you and your sister. You know this. You're both too important to me."

Of course, just as Trevor begins to reply, my boarding number is called.

"I need to go, Trevor. I'm sorry about this mess I've caused."

"Quinn, you can't leave," he states fervently.

"I need to go. I have a movie to start filming, and you have a life to get back to."

"But, Quinn, I—"

"Please, don't." With tears in my eyes, I continue. "Please, I can't do this right now or I'll never get on that plane. And right now I still need to figure things out."

As my boarding number is called again, Trevor anxiously perks up. "Can I message you, at least? Maybe we could arrange something."

With an ache in my chest, I rise onto my toes and press a kiss to Trevor's stubble-covered jaw. He doesn't let me get away with merely a peck. His hand reaches up to my jaw and guides my mouth towards his, pressing his soft lips against mine in a plea. A plea to stay. A plea to give in. A plea to love.

"I'll miss you. Good luck, Trevor."

With a strength I never knew I possessed, I lift my bag and move toward the loading zone, only looking back once as I pass through the gate. The look of anguish on Trevor's face would be enough to break my heart if it wasn't already shattered into a million shards.

I amble onto the plane and find my seat in first class quickly, thankful there were seats available. I clutch the piece of nostalgia in my palm as I rest my head forward with my eyes closed.

The seat beside me dips, and I turn to the older man who's taken the vacant spot.

"Good evening."

"Hello," I respond sullenly, not at all up for a full-fledged conversation.

He settles back into his seat, presses a few buttons on his phone before putting it back in his pocket, and then grabs a magazine from the back of the seat in front of him.

"Business or pleasure?" he asks without looking up.

I think for a moment and then reply truthfully, "Um… both?"

"Did the trip not go well?" he probes as he places the magazine on his lap and turns to me with kind eyes.

"Oh, the trip was fine. Just sad to be going home, that's all."

His chest rises with a single chuckle until his gaze locks on me once more.

"Has anyone ever told you that you're a terrible liar?"

"Yes, I've been told that recently, actually."

"You remind me of someone," he adds, but his eyes don't narrow as if he's trying to place me. "You remind me of my sweet Agatha. That poor woman tried to lie to me all the time when we first met and tell me that she wasn't interested in going steady with me. But I knew better. I could tell by the way she looked at me. So I kept plugging along until she finally caved. Been together for over fifty years now.

"Whatever's botherin' ya, it'll all work out. Everything happens the way it's meant to. Now if ya don't mind, I'm going to get a little shut-eye. I still have one more layover after Los Angeles before I make it back to my sweet lady."

"Thank you…," I press for an introduction.

"Thomas. Thomas Delaney," he replies as he holds out his hand and I respond to his gesture.

"I wish you many more years of happiness, Mr. Delaney."

"Well that's mighty kind of you, Ms. Miller," Thomas adds, surprising me, and I gasp in shock. "What? I may be old, but the missus and I love to go to see motion pictures. You're one of her favorites. And if that tabloid I saw in the newspaper stand has any truth to it, then I'd say you're leaving behind a broken heart."

"You're not wrong. It's all just a blurry mess right now."

"Well, get some shut-eye. Everything is clearer in the morning light."

*

WALKING THROUGH LAX, I tug my hat lower on my head, not wanting the paparazzi to witness my reddened eyes and lack of makeup. Some celebrities use the walk through the airport as another runway, but it's just another reason why I avoid the chance to fly. I don't crave that sort of attention.

Priscilla messages me just as I snag my bag that she's waiting out front with a town car to take me back to my condo. After the bit of sleep I got on the plane, I remembered what Thomas had said before we took off, that everything would seem clearer in the morning light. And he's right. I know I made the best decision to leave; I don't need to come between Izzy and Trevor. They're more than just siblings and twins who share DNA— they're the best of friends and always have been. I'm not worth the mess it would cause in their lives.

My phone rings from a number I don't recognize just as I grab my bag. I hesitate to answer, but something within me tells me I should.

"Hello?"

"Quinn," his deep voice sighs into the phone, as if all is right with the world now that he's heard my voice.

"Trevor? Where are you calling me from?"

"Work. I was just checking to make sure you landed all right. I... I may have been tracking your flight."

"I'm fine and here safe and sound. Did you... did you read my note?"

"No."

"Please. When you get a chance, just read it," I beg as the pounding in my chest intensifies.

"I can't because that means it's over and it's not over, not by a long shot. Our time isn't through yet, Quinn."

"It has to be," I whisper. "My ride is waiting for me, so I need to go."

"Can I... can I text you when I get off work?"

I smile for the first time since my world unraveled the night before. "I'd like that, Trevor. I'll miss you."

"Quinn, wait, I—" Trevor pleads, but I end the call as I step out into the light of the LA morning where Priscilla waits for me.

"Welcome back!" she exclaims joyfully. Then she sees my face and quickly ushers me in the car away from the onlookers.

"What happened to you?" she asks, but my sobs are too overpowering to answer. "Is this about the man in the picture?"

I nod and lean toward her as I continue to cry on her shoulder.

After a few deep breaths, I'm able to right myself and speak.

"I love him."

"I can tell by the way you looked at him in the photo. And it's obvious he feels the same for you. So what's the matter? We can schedule your filming to allow you to fly back every weekend if you want. You know the production team would bend over backward to accommodate you."

Another sob breaks free as I think about how many times I shared myself with Trevor over the past three weeks.

"Did he hurt you?" she asks, and I shake my head before replying, "No. If anything I've hurt him."

"Is it the money thing? A lot of men can't deal with a woman being the breadwinner."

As unladylike as possible, I wipe my nose on the back of my hand and then use my thumbs to wipe away the tears on my cheeks before looking over to my agent and friend.

"I love him and we can't be together because I love his sister just as much."

Priscilla looks at me confused. "Weird love triangle?"

"No," I finally laugh. "They'd been my best friends since I was thirteen and moved to Dale City. Trevor obviously became more to me than just a crush, but my friendship with Izzy is far more important to me. She found out that Trevor and I were sneaking around while I was home and it tore her apart. See, she's known I've crushed on Trevor forever, but she pretty much made me swear that there would never be anything more. I'm sure she did the same with her brother.

"But when I was home, things just… happened. The pull was too strong to fight against it. We made a deal that no feelings would be involved, but obviously that didn't favor well for me. She, um… said she hated me when I showed up at the house, and it broke me even more than losing Trevor, I was losing my best friend. But I could deal with her hating me if she had her brother. I guess as twins they have a special bond, and I would never take that from her. So I left. I took myself out of the equation. Not that it really matters, since I was scheduled to leave tomorrow anyway."

"That's very self-righteous of you, Quinn," she says shamefully. "You know I've always hated when people make decisions for you. It's why I always work so hard to keep you involved with your career so you can take the path you want, not the path I set for you. I thought you would've learned that by now."

"Excuse me?" I ask, eyes wide.

"You heard me. You made a decision for all parties involved and didn't consult anyone. So what if your friend found out and she was upset about you hooking up with her brother? She would've gotten over it eventually. It's not like you broke the law or anything. If she was your friend to begin with and loved you just as much as you love her, then she would've wanted you to be happy, even if that means with her brother.

"And the biggest mistake you've made is that you walked away from love. God, it's like a bad romance novel. How will you feel in a few years when you find out that he's gotten married and had kids? He may be young now, but those things are on the horizon at some point. Geez, Quinn, I don't even know if you can fix this because you're set to leave for filming in two days. You're not even going to be in the same country."

"He… he said he would text me."

"So you can what, have an online romance? Where's the big gesture? Where's your need to fight for him?"

"I left it all back in Dale City," I mumble as I stare out the window.

The drive in LA on a Sunday morning is no better than an early morning on a weekday, car after car packed tight on the freeway like sardines as we slowly make our way to the other side of the city.

As we pull up to my condo, the driver helps unload my bags as Priscilla and I exit.

"I've had the place cleaned this week and the fridge stocked, not that you'll need much of it."

"Priscilla? Thank you. I'll see you in two days."

"Anything for you, girl. Try to get some rest. You're going to need it."

I nod and enter my condo just as Priscilla pulls away in the town car. The phone in my pocket feels like an added weight and I pull it from its confines, toying with the idea of calling Trevor back or even Izzy. Heck, at this point I'd be thrilled to hear Vic's voice.

Instead, as I enter the condo and smell the lemony fresh scent of furniture polish, so different from the crisp airy smell in Dale City, I feel a sense of resolve. I made a choice, a bad one, and now I need to figure out how to fix it.

I toss my bag on the floor, my purse and phone on the countertop of my open concept kitchen, and grab a bottle of water from the fridge. As I turn around, the phone on the counter beckons me and I have to fight against the pull to grab it.

Grateful I'm able to ignore it, I drag my bag with me to the bedroom, quickly unpacking and sorting the laundry.

Adding the most recent phone number to my contacts list, my heart pounds wildly in my chest as I bring up the message app. My fingers shake against the screen, and I have to force myself to take a few calming breaths before I continue.

Using the only two numbers in the app, I type out a quick message.

Me: I love you and I'm sorry.

I shut off the device and place it with my contracts, then shed my clothes and crawl into my neatly made bed before imitating my phone and shutting myself off, from myself and the world.

CHAPTER TWENTY-THREE
Quinn

Two Months Later

HE PLANE FINALLY TOUCHES down back in LAX and I breathe a sigh of relief. It's been two months too long since I've stepped foot in the Golden State. Beside me, Priscilla flips the top of her computer down to power it off and shoves it into her bag. The plane the production team chartered for us assured a nonstop flight from Vancouver, Canada to Los Angeles, and I am forever grateful.

I'm also thrilled to be able to follow up on a few plans I had while I was gone, plans that involve me and my future. Priscilla wasn't too keen on the idea at first, but I think she's warmed up to it with time. Ms. Percell sent me an email through my website announcing her retirement and I took a chance to fund a new community theater group in Dale City, with Ms. Percell as the ringleader, and I couldn't be more thrilled to start the program.

We're escorted off the plane and ushered into a holding area while our bags are retrieved. In the corner, a television airs a local news affiliate, and I use the time to mindlessly catch up on the summary.

The popular entertainment section appears on the screen and I groan as my name flashes across the bottom. The rumor mill surrounding the pictures of me and Trevor has died down, but not completely. I still get the occasional question about him from some of the crew and people I meet in town—mostly those of the female persuasion.

Priscilla's been true to her word and made sure I kept up with Trevor even when I filmed a fourteen-hour day. I had gone from speaking to Izzy every day to not at all. It was quite the adjustment, but I managed. Of course, in the time I've spent away from Izzy and Trevor, I've come to realize how much I love them and how much I miss them in my life.

As Priscilla comes to stand beside me, I notice the stern look on her face and finally focus on the television once more. Pictures of me on set with my costar flash across the screen, questioning a new romance beside one of the photos leaked of Trevor and me.

My heart aches as I imagine him or his sister witnessing these claims.

Speculation over costar romances isn't anything new in the industry, but it's the first time they've targeted me.

"Come on." Priscilla tugs on my arm. "Our bags are ready."

I follow Priscilla into my condo, thankful she had it cleaned before we arrived. A rumble sounds in my gut I move over to the kitchen, searching the upper cabinets until I spy the sleeves of chocolatey goodness. Opening the package of cookies, I take out three and unceremoniously shove them in my mouth like a toddler.

"You look like a starved heathen in here," Priscilla says. "I would've thought you'd learn some manners over the years." She motions for me to share but I hold the package tightly to my chest like it's my prized possession. And after two months of salmon and leafy greens, it most certainly is.

"No, they're mine," I claim, but she doesn't listen. My friend pounces on me, practically knocking me to the floor in her haste to grab the bag of delicious treats. "Stop, you're going to crush my babies!" I shout through the mouthful of Oreos.

Her steady hand reaches between us and grabs a cookie that escaped my hold, and she chants triumphantly as she shoves it into her mouth.

"Fine, you got one. Now get off me."

"Gladly. Now let's talk about your schedule this week."

"My what?" I shove another cookie in my mouth and begrudgingly store the package back in the cabinet. "I'll be back for you," I whisper at the closed door before I turn and meet Priscilla in my living room, where she begins sorting through the mail that was delivered this morning by her assistant.

The box looks ominous as it sits on the floor. Priscilla goes through each rubber-banded bundle and puts aside the important items. It takes her about twenty minutes to sort through everything, and then she hands me an envelope that she claims is the most important.

She tightens her grip when I try to take the envelope. "Quinn, I want you to read this with an open mind. You can say yes or no and I will not judge you." My palm begins to sweat as I consider that something dire rests inside the linen-colored envelope. "Please do what's best for you, not for anyone else."

She finally lets go of the envelope and I hold it in both hands. My name is written in beautiful calligraphy, and it almost pains me to open the flap. As I pull out the heavy cardstock covered by a piece of vellum, my tongue dries and my blood pulses through my veins. Removing the fine parchment, I read the wedding invitation as tears pool in my eyes, making my vision too blurry to focus on the rest of the wording.

"How… how did you know?" I sniffle.

"Because I've been keeping in touch. They have family money, so they obviously pulled this together rather quickly. I don't think most brides can pick out a dress in two months, let alone plan an entire wedding," she admits as she hands me my phone. "I think you leaving was the catalyst to them rushing to the altar. Time is too short to waste."

I stare back down at the invitation and trace over the embossed letters of each name and the date.

"What should I do? I'm not even sure they want me there."

"I don't think you would've been invited if you weren't wanted. And what do you want to do?"

Feeling around in my shorts pocket, I bring out the keyring I've been keeping on me at all times and stare down at the picture. I hadn't realized I was crying until a teardrop falls onto the plastic encasement, and I quickly wipe it away.

"I want to go," I whisper, then turn to Priscilla and say more forcefully, "I want to go."

"I thought that might be your answer. The wedding is tomorrow. I've scheduled you a flight for the morning, and a dress will be waiting for you at the airport with your ride."

"How did you…?"

"Regardless of what took place and what words were exchanged, you love them and want to be there for them. I knew you would say yes. And if you didn't? Well, I was going to take a little trip to see what all the fuss was about," she adds with an oversized grin.

Standing from the sofa, she takes the big box under her arm and carries it to the guest room where she deposited her bags when we arrived.

"Why don't you get some sleep? I'll make sure you're up in the morning."

"Thank you, Priscilla. For everything."

"Don't mention it. What would I do without my favorite client?"

"You'd still have me as your friend."

"And that's why I treat you the way I do. Get some rest."

*

I TAP THE INVITATION against my leg as I sit in the town car, impatiently waiting for us to arrive in Dale City. The red floor-length gown reflects a hint of the sun as it bounces off the satin material.

While I was filming, Priscilla had all of my items from my parents' sent into storage and helped set up an art scholarship for the high school. But as I pass through the city limits, my chest twinges at how much I missed this place, a place I wasn't certain I would ever return to.

"We're here, miss," the driver indicates, and I realize we've parked outside of the church. The same church Izzy, Trevor, and I used to go to every Sunday and sit beside each other in the pews.

My door opens abruptly and I exit the vehicle only to have my name called from the front of the building.

Sue rushes toward me in a beautiful gray dress, expertly making her way down the stairs in her heels.

"You're here! I can't believe you're here. I wasn't sure if you were going to be done filming in time. I'm so relieved."

She starts tugging on my arm, dragging me up the steps until her words finally settle.

"Wait," I say as I dig in my heels. "You're the one who sent me the invitation?"

"Of course, I want all my family together on this joyous day. Come with me, dear. Isabel and Trevor are going to be so shocked to see you!"

As I realize that our turn of events was never relayed to Sue, it's too late to walk away because opening the door before me is Trevor. And not just any Trevor. Trevor in a custom three-piece suit molded to his body like a second skin. I actually gulp.

"I... I need to go, Sue. I don't think I should be here," I apologize as I yank my arm free and rush back toward the front of the building, praying my ride is still waiting. But then I hear my name, and I'm paralyzed from continuing on.

"Quinn?" His voice almost quivers as he calls out. "I'm... I didn't think you'd show."

I finally look up into his piercing green eyes and am struck by the gleam of despair residing in them. Had I done that when I left? Had I quenched the spark that always ignited in my presence? We messaged but nothing ever too deep—I couldn't let our relationship go there again—but that friendship we had as teens was never going to resurface the way it once had been.

"I didn't realize your mother sent the invitation. If I had known I wouldn't have come. I don't want to upset Izzy on her day."

Music begins to play in the church, and Trevor practically stomps his foot in agitation.

"Please stay. I want you to stay. The ceremony is about to start. Would you sit with me?"

"Shouldn't the front just be family?"

"You've always been family, Quinn."

"Okay."

"I'll be out shortly. Just take a seat by Mother. I'll find you."

He kisses my cheek, the soft peck burning itself into my skin, and I'm too stunned to turn away.

"You look beautiful," he adds as he ducks into the room he came from, leaving me alone in the hall with my thoughts.

Twenty minutes later, I'm staring at Izzy in a beautiful white gown while she exchanges vows with Vic. Trevor grasped my hand once he sat down, and I was far too weak to pull away. Now as the ceremony closes, Trevor squeezes my hand gently, enough for me to avert my attention from Izzy to him.

"We need to talk before the reception. Will you come with me?"

"Okay," I respond without hesitation.

Together we stand as Izzy and Vic exit, her eyes widening in surprise and then utter happiness when she sees me standing with her family. I know Trevor and I won't have long to talk before Izzy seeks me out, but I'll take any moment alone with him that I can.

As the couple walks past in their elation, Trevor pulls on my hand and I follow him down the other side of the aisle toward the older part of the church that leads to a small social room.

The motion-activated light flicks on, and Trevor whirls around so abruptly I pin myself to the wall. His chest heaving rapidly, his eyes never leaving my face as he stalks closer. I can feel his warmth through the thin satin of my dress, even from the foot or more distance, and I'm transported back to when we came together in the laundry room at the Dale City Assisted Living Facility.

"I've missed you so goddamn much, Quinn." He wraps one hand around the back of my neck and the other around my waist, dragging my body closer to his.

Trevor pins his mouth against mine and our lips move against each other's in an elusive dance. At this moment I realize how grand of a mistake I made two months ago. We could've worked it out. We could've made things right with Izzy. We could've let our feelings become involved. Maybe I was too scared. Maybe I was too foolish. Maybe I was too naive to realize what I had in my grasp.

I wrap my arms around Trevor's body, clawing at his back, needing to be as close to him as humanly possible. He opens his mouth as my tongue licks at his lower lips, and I accept the invitation wholly.

A knock sounds on the door, quickly followed by Izzy's soft voice. "Quinn? Are you in here?"

She doesn't wait for a response, opening the door just as Trevor pulls his lips away from mine. His hair is messed up, and the skirt of my dress is clenched in his fist. He steps back from me as Izzy walks into the room, quickly followed by Vic, and she rushes toward me.

"I am so surprised to see you," she exclaims as she wraps me in her arms. Her cheek pressed into my neck and shoulder, I feel the wetness of her tears and it quickly triggers my own. I can't believe I thought she needed to choose between me and Trevor. Our friendship was always stronger than that; we could've managed. It may have been iffy for a while, but it would've worked out.

"I'm an idiot," I murmur as I squeeze her back, wanting to keep my friend in my arms forever.

"No, I'm the idiot. I'm so sorry for everything." She steps out of my grasp and begins to pace in front of me, her silken dress swaying between her legs. "For so long, so so long, I was afraid of Trevor hurting you or you hurting him. See, I saw the way you two would look at each other when the other wasn't paying attention, and it tore me up inside. I didn't want to lose my best friend or my brother, and I felt that if you two came together, then I was going to lose you both and our time together. Instead, I suffered by not having Trevor with us all the time, but that meant I got you. And then when I found out what you both did, I was angry. Furious. Because how could the two people I love the most in the world keep this from me and hide it behind my back? But then I fell in love myself, and I understood why you'd want to keep something so personal so private. To keep something just for yourself. It was childish and selfish of me." Turning her glazed-over eyes back to me, she asks, "Will you ever forgive me?"

"I love you, Iz," I reply as I tearfully take her back into my arms.

"I can't believe you stayed away so long," Vic says from his stance beside Trevor, both men devastatingly handsome in their custom-fit tuxedos.

I sniffle once, twice, then admit, "In my defense, I was filming in Canada."

"We know. We're just pulling your leg. We've all been talking with Priscilla. She's the shit, by the way."

"Yes she is," I reply before stepping out of Izzy's embrace. "I don't want to take up your day, so I'm just going to head to the reception. We can catch up later."

"How long are you staying?" Izzy asks.

I draw a blank, not sure if Priscilla booked a room for me in Houston, in town, or frankly at all.

"I, uh… I'm not sure how long I'm staying. Or where, to be honest."

Izzy winks at Trevor and then wraps her hand around Vic's arm.

"Okay, we'll get it all sorted. We'll see you soon."

As they turn to exit, I add, "Izzy, I'm really happy for you."

"Thank you, Quinny."

My nose scrunches up at my distaste for the nickname, and both Izzy and Trevor chuckle.

"Bye, Dizzy Izzy." She's always hated her nickname as much as I hated mine, and I'm not afraid to call her out as she leaves.

The scent of Trevor's cologne fills the air around me as he steps closer. I watch in fascination as he reaches into his suit jacket pocket and reveals a folded piece of paper. My note.

He must see my alarm because he quickly says, "I haven't read it. Even when you told me to, I couldn't. I'm pretty sure I know what it's going to say, and I wasn't prepared to lose you yet. I'm still not ready to lose you. It's been two months and I crave you as much now as I did when you stepped foot back in Dale City not too long ago. You were never just a casual hookup to me, Quinn. You had to have known that. I made a mistake when I made our deal. There was no way I could've kept my feelings from being involved. They've been involved since I was sixteen."

He pauses for a second, looking into my eyes before he asks, "Do you… do you want me to read the note?"

I'm surprised at the casual way he confesses his feelings, but it's just the way Trevor is—straight and to the point. And it's then that I remember he asked about the note, the one wedged between his fingers. My heart lurches at the thought of what I put into that message while I was afraid and hurt. Words I can never take back and wish I had never put to paper to begin with.

"Please don't read it."

His head bobs as he reaches forward and grabs my hand, dragging me behind him out of the room and back toward the front of the church. Outside, the wind picks up, but I feel nothing but the warmth of Trevor's touch on my skin. He guides us over to his Mustang parked in the back corner of the lot. Letting my hand go, he moves to the trunk and reaches inside. Finding what he needs, he makes his way back to me holding a metal plate and a lighter. The flame catches on the paper, and we watch in silence as the remnants of our past burn away into bits of ash and soot to be brushed away effortlessly on the breeze. Kind of like that stupid rule that kept us chained.

"I love you, Quinn," Trevor admits as the last bit of parchment withers away into oblivion.

"I love you too. So much. I beg you to forgive me for running away."

He puts the plate and lighter on the roof of his car and pulls me into his arms.

"There's nothing to forgive, sweetheart. Everything happens for a reason. And like you said, you were filming, so you wouldn't have been around as it is."

"But I left with things such a mess. I left without telling you how I felt."

"I always knew how you felt. Just like you knew about me. We had always said that we couldn't develop feelings for each other, but you can't keep from growing something that was there all along."

"You're right."

"Now the question is how long do you plan to stay?"

"I don't know. What do you think?" I wrap my arms around his neck and lean into his hold.

"Forever. I think you should stay forever."

I pour myself into the kiss. Not just my body, but my heart and soul. I want Trevor to know that forever will never be long enough.

EPILOGUE
Trevor

*T*HE CAR IDLES AS we sit in traffic, police cars corralling us toward a narrow opening in front of the Dolby Theater. Quinn sits beside me, cool as a cucumber, as she reapplies her lipstick from where I had smudged it off about ten minutes ago. Thank goodness for the emergency makeup wipes in her tiny bag.

The deep red on her lips stands out against her pale skin and the fuchsia of her dress. When I came out of the bathroom in the hotel and saw her standing in front of the mirror in the dress, I lost every brain cell in my body. I'd only seen her look as beautiful one other time, when she walked down the aisle toward me a few months back.

Of course, Quinn could wear a potato sack and she would be the most beautiful woman in the room. I love waking up to her each day with her hair mussed, face makeup free, and naked. Well, sometimes she wears one of my shirts to bed, but usually it's gone by the morning.

"Are you nervous?" she asks me as we approach the drop-off area. Now we're only three cars back.

"Naw, I'm not the center of attention so it doesn't bother me. I just want to look good for you."

Her eyes rake over me, and then she gets that hint of a twinkle in her irises that lets me know she's turned on. "You look mighty good in that suit, Trevor."

"Don't give me that look, sweetheart. I'll be tempted to ruin your lipstick again, and I can't promise that your dress is going to remain intact."

Her cute lower lip juts out as she pouts and crosses her arms over her chest.

"Aw, don't be like that," I whisper as I lean in closer and run my nose up the column of her sleek neck. Her small shudder doesn't go unnoticed, and I press my lips to the spot where her neck meets her shoulder.

"Mmm," she moans, and I close my eyes as I take her in.

The car moves again, and I force myself to pull away from Quinn and sit back in the seat, adjusting my erection so I don't embarrass myself and her at the big event.

"How are you feeling?" I ask as we finally pull up to the red carpet.

"Excited. Very excited."

The driver opens the door and I quickly scramble from the car, buttoning my suit jacket as I stand. This is the first time we'll be together as a couple. Though we've been together for just over a year and married for two months, it's been fairly secret since we live back in Dale City.

I assist Quinn as one of her strappy-sandaled feet exits the car. She stands with utter grace and beauty, striking me dumb for just a moment as she smiles warmly at the cameras flashing off in the distance.

How the hell did I get so lucky?

Quinn smiles over at me and presses a light kiss against my lips, causing a ruckus amongst the photographers on the other side of the fence.

"Looks like we're official now," she whispers against my lips.

"Well, the least we can do is give them something to talk about."

The crowd roars as I bend Quinn over my arm and swoop down to claim her as mine in front of the world. Lipstick be damned.

*

"WHAT ARE YOU DOING?" she asks as she unpacks the last of our boxes while I sit lazily on the sofa, rewinding the recording from the Oscars a few nights ago.

In my defense, I just got off a fourteen-hour shift, and Quinn pushed me to the couch the moment I walked in the door with a plate of sandwiches in her hand to make sure I was properly fed. Well, after she let me spread her wide on our new bed, in our new master bedroom, and have my way with her. Not that she complained.

"Well, sweet wife of mine, I'm going to watch my amazing woman accept her first Oscar."

"Again?" she asks as she places the last knickknack on the bookshelf and folds up the box.

"Come here," I beckon and she complies willingly, letting me wrap my arms around her waist as she stands before me. "You are so fucking talented, and I am extremely proud of you. So yes, I'm going to watch it again."

"All right, but I don't need to be in here while you do that. I'm going to go finish unpacking our room."

With the program still paused, I watch as Quinn hops up the stairs, her lean legs flexing under her cutoff shorts with each step. At her publicist's insistence, we bought a new house in a gated community when talk of Quinn's new life in Dale City became public knowledge. Security was key, and this house has it all. It also helped that Vic was able to sell his grandmother's farmhouse, and Izzy used her trust fund to purchase the house down the street because the girls couldn't be far apart since they've made amends. You'd never know that there had been a two-month gap in their friendship.

We don't ever mention the reason behind the "time we do not speak of" to Izzy, ever. Though she seems okay with it now, I know it's still a sore subject. Not the fact that Quinn and I are together; she seems thrilled with it now that she has the sister she's always wanted. It's more that we did it behind her back and lied by omission. Hurting Izzy isn't something I ever want to do again. When she hurts, I hurt.

Turning my attention back to the screen, I press the Play button and watch as the commercial ends and the intro back into the program begins. Last year's winner for best actress stands at the podium and announces each of the nominees. On the screen, I smile like an idiot as Quinn's name is announced and that adorable blush rises on her cheeks at the attention.

The woman goes through the tedious process of announcing the remainder of the nominees and then slides her finger through the black envelope.

"And the winner is... Quinn Miller," the presenter announces dramatically.

The crowd around us stands but Quinn continues sitting, completely shell-shocked. I bent down beside her and whispered in her ear, telling her to get her cute butt up on the stage to get her award or I was dragging her up there over my shoulder. She had jumped up from her seat immediately and wrapped her arms around my neck before rushing toward the stage. How she didn't trip on her dress is beyond me.

I continued to stand while she made her trek, and even as a few of the other audience members sat I still stood. I wanted my girl to know I was there for her, that she deserved every ounce of recognition she was receiving.

"Wow, thank you. I... I honestly didn't think I was going to win this award tonight. I mean, I was nominated alongside actresses I look up to, who I aspire to be. And out of all these greats, you chose me. I'm completely humbled.

"I want to thank all of the amazing cast and crew on the movie. I want to thank Priscilla for being more than just my agent—you're also one of my closest friends. And thank you to Izzy for being the best friend I could ever have asked for. Finally—" She chokes up. "Finally I want to thank my amazing husband, Trevor, for loving me even when I was lost. Thank you for showing me that it's okay to break the rules. I love you."

She blows me a kiss from the stage and the camera pans to me smiling like a loon with misty eyes. But my happiness isn't just from the incredible speech or the fact that she acknowledged me as her husband to all of her colleagues—that secret was already out of the bag. No, my happiness is watching her left hand with that glowing diamond sparkling on her ring finger drape down to cover the baby bump beneath her dress. The little bump no one else will notice, but I know it's there. We heard the tiniest of heartbeats just this past week at her four-month checkup.

Flicking the screen off, I hurriedly make my way up the stairs and find Quinn not unpacking the few remaining boxes in our room, but curled up on her side on the bed with her phone in her hand. I crawl up the end of the bed and over her body as she finishes typing out her text, and then I throw the phone to the opposite side of the bed onto a pillow.

My lips find their favorite spot on her neck just as she says, "The Cunninghams said they could deliver the infamous gazebo this afternoon."

"Did they now?" I ask as I push her onto her back and settle my hips between her legs, making sure not to rest my weight on her stomach.

"Mmhmm. Are you all done watching your video?"

"Yep. Besides, I have something far more important take care of," I admit as I lean in closer, filling my senses with her sweet lavender scent.

Weaving her hands through my hair, she asks, "What's that?"

"You. Always you."

*

STAY IN TOUCH

Newsletter: http://bit.ly/2WokAjS
Author Page:
www.facebook.com/authorreneeharless
Reader Group: http://bit.ly/31AGa3B
Instagram: www.instagram.com/renee_harless
Bookbub: www.bookbub.com/authors/renee-harless
Goodreads: http://bit.ly/2TDagOn
Amazon: http://bit.ly/2WsHhPq
Website: www.reneeharless.com

ACKNOWLEDGEMENTS

Thank you to all of my amazing readers that have patiently waited to get this book into their hands. Between the Lines started off as just an idea I jotted down in my notebook of thoughts and then it persisted to cry out for the book to be written pretty much every day until it was completed. Trevor and Quinn are probably one of my favorite couples because I love a good best friend's brother romance. I hope that you enjoy their story as much as I enjoyed writing it.

Colleen, Crystal, and Amanda – thank you for taking the time to painstakingly read through this book and others numerous times. You all always help me figure out how to make everything work and tie it up with a nice big bow. Your insights are invaluable and I love you all.

Thank you to Hot Tree Editing for allowing me to rush this book over to you and get it back with time to spare. You gave me just a few small days of sanity.

RENEE HARLESS

Jesse, aka Meander, aka my soulmate – I don't have enough words in my vocabulary to tell you how thankful I am for you taking this journey with me. I love you more each day as you support me and watch me grow. It's all about the sunglasses.

Kiddos – thank you for bringing Mommy snacks and giving her precious work time when you know that I'd rather be playing with you. I won't ever get that time back with you but I'm going to make it worth it. You're the best things that have ever happened to me and I love you both very much.

About the Author

Renee Harless is a romance writer with an affinity for wine and a passion for telling a good story.

Renee Harless, her husband, and children live in Blue Ridge Mountains of Virginia. She studied Communication, specifically Public Relations, at Radford University.

Growing up, Renee always found a way to pursue her creativity. It began by watching endless runs of White Christmas- yes even in the summer – and learning every word and dance from the movie. She could still sing "Sister Sister" if requested. In high school, she joined the show choir and a community theatre group, The Troubadours. After marrying the man of her dreams and moving from her hometown she sought out a different artistic outlet – writing.

To say that Renee is a romance addict would be an understatement. When she isn't chasing her toddler or preschooler around the house, working her day job, or writing, she jumps head first into a romance novel.

Reader group: Renee Harless' Risque Readers
https://www.facebook.com/groups/reneeharlessrisquereaders/
Facebook: facebook.com/authorreneeharless
Amazon: www.amazon.com/Renee-Harless/e/B00VAHGAWE
Bookbub: www.bookbub.com/authors/renee-harless
Newsletter: www.reneeharless.com/newsletter
Instagram: @Renee_harless
Twitter: @Renee_harless
Snapchat: @renee_harless

www.ingramcontent.com/pod-product-compliance
Lightning Source LLC
Chambersburg PA
CBHW071159100726
47908CB00002B/444